Snow Falling on Cedars

DAVID GUTERSON

Level 6

Retold by Christopher Tribble
Series Editors: Andy Hopkins and Jocelyn Potter

Pearson Education Limited

Edinburgh Gate, Harlow,
Essex CM20 2JE, England
and Associated Companies throughout the world.

ISBN: 978-1-4058-8273-6

This adaptation first published in the Longman Fiction Series 1997
by arrangement with Bloomsbury Publishing Limited, London
First published by Penguin Books Ltd 1999
This edition first published 2008

3 5 7 9 10 8 6 4 2

Typeset by Graphicraft Ltd, Hong Kong
Set in 11/14pt Bembo
Printed in China
SWTC/02

Published by Pearson Education Ltd in association with
Penguin Books Ltd, both companies being subsidiaries of Pearson Plc

For a complete list of the titles available in the Penguin Readers series please write to your local
Pearson Longman office or to: Penguin Readers Marketing Department, Pearson Education,
Edinburgh Gate, Harlow, Essex CM20 2JE, England.

Contents

Introduction

The heart of any other, because it had a will, would remain ever mysterious.

Ishmael . . . understood this, too: that accident ruled every corner of the universe except the chambers of the human heart.

Snow Falling on Cedars in set on the island of San Piedro. The island is home to people whose families have come from other countries to find a new and better life in the north west of the United States. But these people have brought their old ways with them. The various groups on the island keep apart from each other and, over the years, many social problems have developed. People of different races fail to understand each other. Sometimes they do not even try.

The islanders have two main occupations. One is salmon fishing. The work is hard and the fishermen have to work alone in difficult conditions. The salmon swim into nets and are trapped. So too, the fishermen of San Piedro are trapped in their own way of life and family backgrounds. Others on the island own land on which they farm strawberries. The work is a little easier than fishing and the landowners feel more secure.

The story begins in the autumn of 1954. The Second World War has ended, but the memories of it remain. The Japanese living on San Piedro are not trusted because no one can forget how Japan attacked the Americans in the Pacific. So when Carl Heine, a fisherman from a German family, is found dead on his boat in mysterious circumstances, many people are willing to accuse his Japanese neighbour of murder.

Evidence is found that seems to point to the guilt of the fisherman, Kabuo Miyamoto, and he is brought to trial in the local court in the island's main town. In court, Kabuo sits straight and remains silent. He reminds some people of a Japanese soldier, but his enemies choose to forget that Kabuo fought in the United States army, not for the Japanese.

Ishmael Chambers runs the local newspaper and it is his task to report honestly on the events leading up to the trial and the trial itself. But Ishmael has a personal problem with Kabuo – and with Japanese people generally. His search for truth is a struggle, but he finally understands that although we can never really understand other people, however well we think we know them, the human heart can never be ignored.

The novel was made into a successful film in 1999. David Guterson has now written three other books: *The Drowned Son* (1996), *East of the Mountains* (1999), and *Our Lady of the Forest* (2003).

David Guterson was born in Seattle, Washington state, in the north-west of the United States, in 1956. He was educated at the University of Washington and has degrees in Literature and Creative Writing. But as Guterson himself explains, he loves and needs the beautiful countryside of Washington state. He is not happy unless he is free to walk across the land he loves and enjoy the beauty of its trees and mountains.

Guterson therefore set his first novel, *Snow Falling on Cedars*, in an area which is as isolated and beautiful as Guterson's own home. The trial takes place against the background of the first snows of winter. The beautiful cedars are covered for a time by the snow, just as the truth is hidden. The snow continues to play a part as the story develops, as does the fog out at sea. At the end of the book, the snow covers everything with its perfect whiteness.

The novel was first published in 1994 and was an immediate success. It had taken the author ten years to write, as he was also teaching in a local school at the time. Guterson has said that the writing of this book was strongly influenced by Harper Lee's *To Kill a Mocking Bird*, which was published in 1960. This important novel, set in the American South of the time, is a story about a black man accused of a sexual attack on a white girl. Atticus Finch, the young man's lawyer, tries to make sure that the accused has a fair trial, but the time and the place are against this and the story has an unhappy ending. The story is fiction, but it explores important moral issues of racism, justice and individual responsibility. Guterson, too, believes that fiction should help people to understand the society they live in and to take the responsibility of making it a better place. He also thinks that the moral truths that he writes about are the same today as they always were.

People in Guterson's book have long memories. The historical background of the story is therefore very important. Japanese people were first been invited to work in the United States in the early years of the twentieth century. They were promised work and good money. Although at first their stay was temporary, many settled in Washington state and became fishermen and farmers. These people could not own land, but their children could. The Japanese worked hard and did well. They thought of themselves as Americans, but they kept their old traditions. Of course, they looked different from their neighbours and they were often disliked because of it.

The Second World War began in Europe in 1939. At first, the United States did not fight, but on 7th December 1941, the Japanese attacked the American military base at Pearl Harbor on Hawaii, in the Pacific. The United States immediately declared war on Japan and, as a result, all the Japanese living in the States were put in camps until the end of the war in 1945. Strangely, the Germans and Italians, whose countries were also fighting the States, were allowed to stay in their own homes.

Ten years later, these unhappy memories still influence the way people on San Piedro think about each other.

Chapter 1 The Trial Begins

The accused man, Kabuo Miyamoto, sat proudly upright, as if trying to distance himself from his own trial. He showed no emotion – not even the smallest movement of his eyes. He was dressed in a white shirt worn buttoned to the throat and grey, neatly pressed trousers. His body, especially the neck and shoulders, spoke of great physical strength. Kabuo's features were smooth and sharp edged; his hair had been cut close to his skull so that the muscles seemed to stand out. As the charge against him was read, his dark eyes looked straight ahead, showing no emotion.

The eighty-five citizens in the public part of the court were strangely quiet and thoughtful in that small over-heated room. Most of them had known Carl Heine, now buried up on Indian Knob Hill, a salmon fisherman with a wife and three children. Most had dressed today with the same care they took on Sundays before going to church, and since Judge Llewellyn Fielding's courtroom, however simple, mirrored in their hearts the holiness of their prayer houses, they behaved with church-going quietness. The jurors, too, sat quietly as they tried to make sense of matters. The men were all dressed in coats and ties. The women all wore Sunday dresses.

Snow fell that morning outside the tall, narrow courthouse windows. A wind from the sea threw snow against the glass. Beyond the courthouse the town of Amity Harbor spread along the island shore towards a few ageing, wind-whipped houses. The snow made it difficult to see the clean lines of the green, cedar-covered hills. The accused man watched the falling snow. He had been shut away from the world in the county prison for seventy-seven days – the last part of September, all of October and all of

1

November, the first week of December. There was no window anywhere in his cell through which the autumn light could come to him. He had missed autumn, he realized now – it had passed already, disappeared. The snowfall, which he saw out of the corners of his eyes, struck him as being endlessly beautiful.

Five thousand people lived on San Piedro, an island named by the sailors on a lost Spanish ship in the year 1603. Amity Harbor, the island's only town, was home to fishing ships and one-man gill-netting boats. It was a rainy, wind-beaten sea village which had seen better times. On winter nights its steep streets lay broad and empty under the rain.

San Piedro also had a green beauty, with enormous cedar-covered hills rising and falling to the north and the south. The island homes were built among fields of grass, grain and strawberries. Fences lined the careless roads which slid beneath the shadows of the trees and past the fields. Here and there an islander cut timber on his own, leaving sweet-smelling piles of dust at the side of the road. The beaches shone with smooth stones and seawater. All along the coast of San Piedro was an endless series of perfect natural harbours, each with its pleasant mixture of boats and summer homes.

Ishmael Chambers, the local reporter, sat among his colleagues from out-of-town, feeling unhappy and uncomfortable about their lack of seriousness. He was a man of thirty-one with a hardened face, a tall man with the eyes of an ex-soldier. He had only one arm; the left was cut off ten inches below the shoulder joint, so that he wore the sleeve of his coat pinned up. The accused man, Kabuo, was somebody he knew, somebody he'd gone to high school with, and he couldn't bring himself, like the other reporters, to remove his coat at Kabuo's murder trial.

At ten minutes before nine that morning Ishmael had spoken with the accused man's wife on the second floor of the Island County Courthouse. 'Are you all right?' he'd said to her, but she'd answered by turning away from him. 'Please,' he'd said. 'Please, Hatsue.' She'd turned her eyes on his then. Ishmael would find later, long after the trial, that their darkness would fill his memory of these days. He would remember how her hair had been tied into a precise black knot against the back of her neck. She had not been exactly cold to him, not exactly hateful, but he'd felt her distance. 'Go away,' she'd said in a whisper, and then for a moment she'd looked at him with wide open eyes. He was uncertain afterwards what her eyes had meant – punishment, sorrow, pain? 'Go away,' repeated Hatsue Miyamoto. Then she'd turned her eyes, once again, from his.

'Don't be like this,' said Ishmael.

'Go away,' she'd answered.

'Hatsue,' said Ishmael. 'Don't be like this.'

'Go away,' she'd said again.

Now he sat facing the wind-driven snowfall, which had already begun to silence the streets outside the courthouse windows. He hoped it would snow without stopping and bring to the island the impossible winter purity, so rare and perfect, he remembered from his youth.

Chapter 2   The Discovery

The first witness called by the prosecutor that day was the county sheriff, Art Moran. He told the court how his deputy, Abel Martinson, had radioed in to say that Carl Heine's fishing boat, the *Susan Marie*, was in White Sand Bay, and no one was at the wheel. When he and his deputy had reached it, they found that all the boat's lights were burning – something that struck the sheriff as strange – but there was no one on board.

The lamp over the ship's wheel had been left on; sunlight shone on the right-hand wall. The scene worried Art, with its sense of extreme, too-silent tidiness. A sausage hanging from a wire swung a little with the movement of the boat; otherwise, nothing moved. No sound could be heard except now and again a small distant noise from the radio set. Art, noticing it, began to turn the radio controls for no other reason than that he didn't know what else to do. He simply did not know what to do.

'This is bad,' said Abel.

'We'd better take a look,' said Art. 'See if there's any sign of him.'

The search that the two men made revealed nothing, although they saw that the salmon net was still in the water.

'Well, look,' said Abel Martinson. 'Let's get his net in, Art.'

'I suppose we'd better,' sighed Art. 'All right. We'd better do it, then. But we'll do it one step at a time.'

As they brought the net in to the boat, the morning light became brighter, gained greater depth, and lay in a clean silver sheet across the bay. The only other boat in sight was travelling parallel to the tree-lined shore a quarter mile away, full of children in life jackets. 'They're innocent,' thought Art.

He looked across at Abel. 'Get over there with the line,' he said softly. 'I'll bring her up real slow. You may need to clear some fish, so be ready.'

Abel Martinson nodded.

They had picked two dozen salmon from the net and three or four other kinds of fish, when Carl Heine's face showed. For a brief moment Art thought that Carl's face was the sort of thing men imagined they saw when at sea – or hoped it was this – but then, as the net came in, Carl's bearded throat appeared, too, and the face completed itself. There was Carl's face turned up towards the sunlight, and the water from Carl's hair dripped in silver strings to the sea; and now clearly it was Carl's face, his mouth open – Carl's face. Up he came, hanging by the left button of his rubber trousers from the net he'd made his living from; his

4

T-shirt, filled with seawater, stuck to his chest and shoulders. He hung heavily with his legs in the water, a salmon struggling in the net beside him, the skin of his neck, just above the highest waves, icy but brilliant pink. He appeared to have been boiled in the sea.

Abel Martinson was sick. He leaned over the side of the boat, cleared his throat and was sick again, this time more violently.

'All right, Abel,' Art said. 'You get control of yourself.'

The deputy did not reply. He wiped his mouth with a cloth. He breathed heavily and cleared his mouth into the sea a half-dozen times. Then, after a moment, he dropped his head and banged his left hand against the side. 'Oh my God,' he said.

'I'll bring him up slow,' answered Art. 'You keep his head back away from the side, Abel. Get control of yourself. Keep his head back and away now.'

But in the end they had to pull Carl fully into the folds of his net. They wrapped the net around him so that his body was held by it. In this manner they brought Carl Heine up from the sea – Abel pulling him over the net roller while Art tried to make sure the body did not bang against the side of the boat. They laid him, together, on the wooden boards. In the cold salt water he had stiffened quickly; his right foot had frozen solidly over his left, and his arms, locked at the shoulders, were fixed in place with the fingers curled. His mouth was open. His eyes were open, too, but Art saw how they'd turned backwards and now looked inwards. The blood vessels in the whites of his eyes had burst; there were two red balls in his head. Abel Martinson stared.

Art found that he could not bring any professionalism to this problem. He simply stood by, like his 24-year-old deputy, thinking the thoughts a man thinks at such a time about the ugly certainty of death. They simply stood looking down at Carl's dead body, a thing that had silenced both of them.

'He banged his head,' whispered Abel Martinson, pointing to a wound Art hadn't noticed in Carl Heine's fair hair. 'Must have banged it against the side going over.' Sure enough, Carl Heine's skull had been pushed in just above his left ear. The bone had broken and left a hollow place on the side of his head. Art Moran turned away from it.

Chapter 3   The Defence

Nels Gudmundsson, Kabuo Miyamoto's lawyer, rose with the slowness and careful awkwardness of old age to question Art Moran. He cleared his throat and hooked his thumbs in his jacket pockets. At seventy-nine, Nels was blind in his left eye and could only make out shades of light and darkness, although the right eye seemed bright and sharp in compensation.

'Sheriff,' he said. 'Good morning.'

'Good morning,' replied Art Moran.

'I just want to make sure I'm hearing you right on a couple of matters,' said Nels. 'You say the lights on this boat, the *Susan Marie*, were all on? Is that right?'

'Yes,' said the sheriff, 'they were.'

'In the cabin, too?'

'That's right.'

'The mast lights?'

'Yes.'

'The net lights? All of them?'

'Yes, sir,' said Art Moran.

'Thank you,' Nels said. 'I thought that was what you said, all right. That they were all on. All the lights.'

He paused and for a moment seemed to study his hands.

'You say it was foggy on the night of 15th September?' Nels asked. 'Is that what you said, Sheriff?'

'Yes.'

'Thick fog?'

'Absolutely.'

'What time did you get up, Sheriff? Do you remember? On the sixteenth?'

'I got up at five. At five o'clock.'

'And was the fog still there?'

'Yes, it was.'

'So it was still foggy in the morning, then.'

'Yes. Until nine or so.'

'Until around nine,' Nels Gudmundsson repeated.

'That's right,' replied Art Moran.

Nels Gudmundsson raised his chin, fingered his tie, and pulled experimentally at the loose skin on his neck – a habit of his when he was thinking.

'Out there on the *Susan Marie*,' he said, 'the engine started right up, Sheriff? When you went to start it you had no trouble?'

'Right away,' said Art Moran. 'No trouble at all.'

'With all those lights on, Sheriff? Batteries still strong?'

'Must have been. Because she started with no trouble.'

'Did that strike you as odd, Sheriff? Do you remember? That with all those lights on, the batteries could still turn the engine over with no trouble, as you say?'

'Didn't think about it at the time,' said Art Moran. 'So "No" is the answer – it didn't strike me as odd, at least not then.'

'And does it strike you as odd now?'

'A little,' said the sheriff. 'Yes.'

Nels made his way to the evidence table, selected a folder, and brought it to Art Moran.

'Could you turn to page seven, please?'

The sheriff did so.

'Now, could you read for the court item number twenty-seven?'

'Of course,' said Art Moran. 'Item twenty-seven. A spare D-8 battery.'

'A spare D-8 battery.' said Nels. 'Thank you. A D-8. Would you turn now to item forty-two, sheriff? And read one more time for the court?'

'Item forty-two,' replied Art Moran. 'D-8 and D-6 batteries in battery holder.'

'A 6 and an 8?' Nels said.

'Yes.'

'I did some measuring down at the boat store,' said Nels. 'A D-6 is wider than a D-8 by an inch. It wouldn't fit into the *Susan Marie*'s battery holder, Sheriff – it was an inch too large for that.'

'He'd changed things a bit,' Art explained. 'The side of the holder was banged away to make room for a D-6.'

'He'd banged out the side of the battery holder?'

'Yes.'

'You could see this?'

'Yes.'

'A piece of metal that had been banged aside?'

'Yes.'

'Soft metal?'

'Yes. Soft enough. It'd been banged back to make room for a D-6.'

'To make room for a D-6,' Nels repeated. 'But Sheriff, didn't you say that the spare was a D-8?'

'The spare was dead,' Art Moran said. 'We tested it after we brought the boat in. It was carrying no electricity, Mr Gudmundsson. None at all.'

'The spare was dead,' Nels repeated. 'So, to sum up, you found on the boat a dead spare D-8 battery, a working D-8, and beside it a working D-6 that was, in fact, too large for the existing space and which had forced someone to do some refitting? Some banging at a soft metal part?'

'All correct,' said the sheriff.

'Now,' said Nels Gudmundsson. 'Please turn to page twenty-seven of your report? Your list of items on the defendant's boat? And read for the court item twenty-four, please?'

Art Moran turned the pages. 'Item twenty-four,' he said after a while. 'Two D-6 batteries.'

'Two D-6s on Kabuo Miyamoto's boat,' Nels said. 'And did you find a spare, Sheriff?'

'No, we didn't. It isn't in the list.'

'The defendant had no spare battery on his boat? He'd gone out fishing without one?'

'Apparently, yes, sir, he did.'

'Well, then,' Nels said. 'Two D-6s in the battery holder and no spare to be found. Tell me, Sheriff... These D-6s on the defendant's boat. Were they the same sort of D-6 you found in the deceased's battery holder on board the *Susan Marie*? The same size? The same make?'

'Yes,' replied the sheriff. 'All D-6s. The same battery.'

'So the D-6 in use on the deceased's boat could have made a perfect spare for the defendant's batteries?'

'I suppose so.'

'But, as you say, the defendant had no spare on board. Is that right?'

'Yes.'

'All right, Sheriff,' Nels said. 'Let me ask you about something else, if you don't mind, for a moment. Tell me – when you brought Carl Heine's body in, was there some sort of trouble? When you pulled him up from the sea in his fishing net?'

'Yes,' said Art Moran. 'I mean, he was heavy. And, well, his lower half – his legs and feet – they wanted to slide out of the net. His legs were hanging in the water, you understand. His legs weren't quite in the net.'

'So you had some trouble,' Nels said.

'A little, yes.'

'Sheriff,' said Nels Gudmundsson, 'is it possible the deceased hit his head on the side of the boat as you were bringing him in? Or somewhere else? Is it possible?'

'I don't think so,' said Art Moran. 'I would have seen it if he did.'

'You don't think so,' Nels said. 'Or to put it another way, do you have any uncertainty at all about this? That in doing this difficult job of bringing in a drowned man of 235 pounds − is it possible, Sheriff Moran, that he banged his head sometime after his death? Is that possible?'

'Yes,' said Art Moran. 'Possible. I guess it is − but not likely.'

Nels Gudmundsson turned towards the jury. 'No more questions,' he said. And with a slowness that embarrassed him − because as a young man he had been fit and active − he made his way back to his seat at the defendant's table, where Kabuo Miyamoto sat watching him.

Chapter 4   Ishmael Chambers

When the judge left the court for the morning break, and while the jury went out to get coffee, the accused man, Kabuo Miyamoto, leaned to his right while Nels Gudmundsson spoke into his ear. Ishmael Chambers found a seat and sat tapping his pencil against his bottom lip. Like others on San Piedro Island, he'd first heard about the death of Carl Heine on the afternoon of September 16th. Ishmael Chambers did not believe the news at first. Still disbelieving, he phoned the sheriff's office and asked if Carl Heine had drowned. They told him that it was true, that he'd hit his head on something.

On that morning, when he heard the news, Ishmael Chambers put down the receiver and sat with his forehead held in his hand, remembering Carl Heine from high school. They had played on the football team together. He remembered riding the team bus with Carl to a game against Bellingham in the autumn of '41. They rode wearing their sports clothes, each boy carrying his own equipment. He remembered how Carl had looked sitting beside him with his team shirt open at his thick German neck. He had stared out of the bus windows at the passing fields. 'Chambers,' he'd said, 'you see the birds there?'

Ishmael slid a notepad into the pocket of his trousers and left his office, wondering why he was still living on San Piedro. After the war, a man of twenty-three with one arm, he'd been pleased to leave the island and to attend college in Seattle, where he had rented a room and taken history classes. He had not been particularly happy in this period, but that did not make him different from other ex-soldiers. He was aware of his pinned-up sleeve, and felt troubled because it troubled other people. Since they could not forget about it, neither could he. He felt foolish if he went to bars and drank beer and played games. He felt more comfortable at a table in the back of Day's Restaurant on University Way, where he drank coffee and read his history.

The next autumn Ishmael took up American literature. Reading Mark Twain and other American classics, he came to the conclusion that books were a good thing, but that was all they were and nothing else – they couldn't put food on his table. And so Ishmael turned to journalism.

His father, Arthur, had worked in the forests on San Piedro at Ishmael's age and the *San Piedro Review*, a four-page weekly newspaper, was the invention of his early twenties. With his savings he acquired a printing press, a camera, and a cold, low-ceilinged office behind a fish-processing store, from which base Arthur started to report local stories and matters of national importance. He also learned how to print the paper himself, laying out the pages in an old-fashioned typeface, with delicate lines separating the columns and headlines.

In 1919 Arthur married a Seattle woman, fair-haired and dark-eyed, and settled down to the business of raising children, though they had only one. They built a house at South Beach with a view of the sea and cleared a path to the beach. Arthur became an expert vegetable gardener, an observer of island life, and gradually a small-town newspaperman in the truest sense: he came to recognize the opportunity his words provided for influence, fame and service.

Ishmael remembered running the old green printing press with his father every Tuesday evening. A loyalty to his profession and its principles had made Arthur, over the years, increasingly careful in his speech and actions, and increasingly insistent on the truth in all his reporting. He was, his son remembered, deeply and carefully honest, and though Ishmael might try to match his standards, there was nevertheless this matter of the war – this matter of the arm he'd lost – that made such honesty difficult. Ishmael didn't like very many people any more, or very many things. He would have preferred not to be this way, but there it was, he was like that. His lack of trust in the world – an ex-soldier's lack of trust – was a thing that worried him all the time. It seemed to him after the war that the world was completely altered. It was not even a thing you could explain to anybody. People appeared enormously foolish to him. He understood that they were only living bags full of strings and liquids. He had seen the insides of dead people. He knew, for instance, what brains looked like coming out of somebody's head. Normal life seemed worryingly ridiculous. He didn't exactly want to push people away, it was just that he had this unhappy view of the world, no matter how much he might not want it, and it made him suffer.

Later, when he was no longer so young and he was back home on San Piedro Island, this view of things began to change. He learned to seem friendly to everyone – even though this hid his true feelings. Gradually Ishmael came to view himself as a disappointed one-armed man with a pinned-up sleeve, past thirty and unmarried. It was not so bad then, even if it was not honest, and he was not so angry as he had once been in Seattle.

His mother, who was fifty-six and lived alone in the old family house on the south end of the island – the house where Ishmael had lived as a child – had pointed out to him when he'd come home from the city that his inability to like the world did not suit him, brought out the worst in him. His father before him had been the same, she said, and it had been wrong in him, too.

'He loved people dearly and with all his heart, but he disliked most human beings,' she'd told Ishmael. 'You're the same, you know. You're your father's son.'

◆

By the time Ishmael arrived at the Amity Harbor docks, Art Moran was standing talking to half a dozen fishermen – William Gjovaag, Marty Johansson and others. They were gathered in front of Carl Heine's boat. Today there were a lot of seagulls in the harbour. Fishermen sometimes shot at them, but for the most part the gulls were left alone.

San Piedro fishermen – in those days, at least – went out in the evening to work the seas. Most of them were gill-netters, men who travelled into lonely waters and dropped their nets where the salmon swam. The nets hung down like curtains in the dark water and the salmon, unsuspecting, swam into them.

A gill-netter passed his night hours in silence, rocking on the sea and waiting patiently. It was important that he had the right character for this, otherwise his chances of success were small. At times the salmon ran in such narrow waters that men had to fish for them in sight of one another, in which case arguments happened, but far more often a man was alone all night and had no one to argue with. Some who had tried this lonely sort of life had given up and joined the crews of deep-sea fishing boats.

Gradually Anacortes, a town on the mainland, became home to the big boats with crews of four or more, Amity Harbor home to one-man gill-netters. It was something San Piedro prided itself on, the fact that its men had the courage to fish alone even in bad weather. San Piedro people felt that fishing alone was better than fishing in other ways, so that the sons of fishermen, when they dreamed at night, dreamed of going out in their lonely boats and pulling great salmon from the sea in their nets.

Ishmael Chambers knew, as he approached the men gathered before the *Susan Marie*, that he was not a part of this group, that furthermore he made his living with words and was thus not trusted by them. On the other hand, he had the advantage of having been wounded in the war; the advantage of any ex-soldier whose war years are for ever a mystery to those who did not fight. These were things that the fishermen could appreciate and that lessened their distrust of a man who sat behind a typewriter all day.

They nodded at him and included him in their circle.

'Did you see Susan Marie?' asked Ishmael.

'I did,' said Art.

'Three kids,' said Ishmael. 'What's she going to do?'

'I don't know,' said the sheriff.

'She say anything?'

'Not a word.'

'Well, what's she going to say?' put in William Gjovaag. 'What can she say?'

'Do you know what happened?' he asked the sheriff.

'That's just what I'm trying to find out,' said Art Moran.

Apparently, Heine had been seen the previous evening heading for the fishing grounds, but no one had seen him after eight o'clock. It had been a foggy night and the fishing had been poor. Most of the men had moved to another part of the coast.

It was not until they'd left the docks altogether and turned onto Harbor Street that Art Moran talked directly to Ishmael. 'Look,' he said, 'I know what you're thinking. You want to do an article that says Sheriff Moran suspects something and is investigating, am I right?'

'I don't know what to say,' said Ishmael Chambers. 'I don't know anything about it yet. I was hoping you'd tell me.'

'Well, sure, I'll tell you,' said Art Moran. 'But you've got to promise me something first. You won't say anything about an investigation, all right? If you want to quote me on the subject, here's my quote: Carl Heine drowned by accident, or something like that, you make it up, but don't say anything about an investigation. Because there isn't one.'

'You want me to lie?' asked Ishmael Chambers. 'I'm supposed to make up what you say?'

'Off the record?' said the sheriff. 'OK, there's an investigation. Some tricky, funny little facts floating around – could mean anything, where we stand now. Could be murder, could be an accident – could be anything. We just don't know yet. But if you go telling everyone that on the front page of the *Review*, we aren't ever going to find out. As far as the *San Piedro Review* is concerned there is no "investigation", OK? Let's you and I be clear on that.'

'I'm clear on it,' said Ishmael. 'All right, I'll quote you as calling it an accident. You keep me up to date on what develops.'

'A deal,' said Art. 'A deal. If I find anything, you're the first to know. How's that? You got what you want now?'

'Not yet,' said Ishmael. 'I've still got this story to write. So will you give me a few answers about this accident?'

'I will,' said Art Moran. 'What do you want to know?'

Chapter 5 After a Death

The next witness was Horace Whaley, the Island County Coroner. He had been at his desk doing paperwork on the morning of September 16th when the phone beside him rang. He felt upset as he brought the receiver to his ear; since the war he could not do too many things at once and at the moment, busier than he liked to be, did not wish to speak to anyone. It was under these circumstances that he heard about the death of Carl Heine.

The sheriff and his deputy had laid the body on its back on Horace Whaley's examination table, its booted feet sticking out from under a white ex-navy sheet. Horace Whaley turned back one of these sheets and looked in at Carl Heine. The jaw had set open, he saw, and the dead man's tongue had disappeared down the stiff throat. A large number of blood vessels had broken in the whites of the dead man's eyes. Horace pulled the sheet over Carl Heine again. Art Moran then told him how the body had been found and that he would now have to go and give the news to Carl Heine's wife, Susan Marie. He would leave the deputy with Horace to give any help that might be needed.

When he was gone Horace looked at Carl Heine's face again, letting Art's young deputy wait in silence, then washed his glasses at the sink. 'Tell you what,' he said at last. 'You go on across the hall and sit in my office, all right? There's some magazines in there and a radio and some coffee if you want it. And if I need your help, I'll call for you. Sound fair enough, Deputy?'

'OK,' said Abel Martinson. 'You call me.'

He picked up his hat and carried it out with him. 'Stupid kid,' Horace said to himself. Then he dried his steel-framed glasses and got his white coat on. He removed the sheets from Carl Heine, and then, very carefully, using angled scissors, cut away the rubber overalls, dropping pieces of them in a cloth bag. When the overalls were gone he began on the shirt and cut away Carl Heine's work trousers and underwear and pulled off Carl's boots and socks, out of which seawater ran. In Carl Heine's left front pocket were a watch that had stopped at 1.47 and a ball of string. An empty knife-holder was still attached to his belt.

The body – despite the two hours it had spent in transport – had not softened noticeably, Horace observed. It was pink, the colour of salmon flesh, and the eyes had turned back in the head. It was also exceedingly powerful, heavy and thick-muscled, the chest broad, and Horace Whaley could not help thinking that here was an extraordinary male specimen, six foot three and two hundred and thirty-five pounds, bearded, fair-haired and built to last like a well-constructed house.

The Island County Coroner coughed twice, dryly, and began, consciously, for this would be necessary, to think of Carl Heine, a man he knew, as 'the deceased' and not as Carl Heine. The deceased's right foot had locked itself behind the left, and Horace now forced himself to free it. It was necessary to pull hard enough to tear muscles in the deceased's leg, and this Horace Whaley did.

His main concern now, as he stood looking at Carl Heine's unclothed form, was to discover the precise cause of Carl's death, or rather to discover how the deceased had become the deceased. For to think of the piece of flesh before him as Carl, Horace reminded himself, would make doing what he had to do difficult; although Carl Heine had not been a likeable man, neither was he a bad sort. Because of this, he must think of Carl as the deceased, a bag of tubes and soft parts, and not as the man who had so recently brought his son in to have a cut treated; otherwise the job could not be done.

Horace Whaley put his right hand against the stomach of the dead man. He placed his left hand over it and began to pump in the manner of someone attempting to help a victim of drowning. And as he did so something like soapy cream, though pink with

17

blood from the lungs, came out of the deceased's mouth and nose. Horace stopped and inspected this. It was a result, Horace knew, of air, body liquids and seawater all mixed by breathing, and meant the deceased had been alive when he went under the water. He had not died first and then been thrown beneath the waves. Carl Heine had gone in breathing.

But had he been unconscious before going into the water, dying painlessly as his brain was denied oxygen, or had he died a painful death by drowning? It was while considering this question that he noticed – how had he missed it before? – the wound to the skull over the dead man's left ear. 'Well, what kind of a doctor am I . . . ?' he said aloud.

He cut hair out of the way until the shape of this wound emerged cleanly. The bone had been broken and gone inwards over an area of about four inches. The skin had split open, and from the wound a tiny piece of pink brain material stuck out. Whatever had caused this wound, a narrow, flat object about two inches wide, had left its shape in the deceased man's head. It was precisely the sort of wound Horace had seen at least two dozen times in the Pacific war, the result of close fighting, hand to hand, and made by the handle of a gun. The Japanese field soldier, trained in the art of *kendo*,★ or stick fighting, was exceptionally efficient at killing in this manner. And the majority of Japs,† Horace recalled, killed by striking over the left ear, swinging in from the right.

Horace took a sharp blade and pushed it into the deceased's head. He pressed towards the bone and guided it through the hair, cutting a semicircle across the top of the deceased's skull literally from ear to ear. It was skilfully and steadily done, like

★ kendo: a traditional form of fighting, now a character-building sport.

† Japs: an offensive word for Japanese people, which shows the speaker's dislike or disrespect.

drawing a curved line with a pencil across the top of the dead man's head. In this manner he was able to pull back the dead man's face as though it were the skin of an orange and turn his forehead inside out so that it rested against his nose.

Horace pulled down the back of the head, too, then laid his knife in the sink and brought out a saw from his instrument cupboard. He then began the work of cutting through the bone of the dead man's skull. When Art Moran returned half an hour later, Horace Whaley was finishing this task.

Art stood there watching while Horace, in his white coat, worked carefully with his saw. He forced himself to watch, hating having to do it but knowing that he must, while Horace removed the top of the dead man's skull and placed it beside the dead man's shoulder.

'This is called the *dura mater*.'* Horace pointed with his knife. 'See? Right under his skull? This right here is the *dura mater*.'

He took the remains of the dead man's head and turned it to the left.

'Come over here, Art,' he said.

The sheriff seemed aware of the necessity of doing so; nevertheless, he didn't move. Horace Whaley knew that the sheriff did not want to see what was inside Carl Heine's head. 'It'll just take a minute,' Horace urged him. 'One quick look, Art. So you can see what we're facing. I wouldn't ask if it wasn't important.'

Horace showed Art Moran how the blood had flowed into the *dura mater* and the tear in it where the piece of brain came through. 'He got hit pretty hard with something fairly flat, Art. Makes me think of a type of wound I saw a few times in the war. One of those *kendo* strikes the Japs used.'

'*Kendo*?' said Art Moran.

* dura mater: one of the three strong layers of tissue which surround the brain.

19

'Stick fighting,' Horace explained. 'Japs are trained in it from when they're kids. How to kill with sticks.'

'Ugly,' said the sheriff.

Horace also showed the sheriff three small pieces of the deceased's skull that had stuck in the tissue of his brain.

'That what killed him?' Art asked. 'Can you find out?'

'Maybe.'

'When?'

'I have to look inside his chest, Art. At his heart and lungs. And even that might not tell me much.'

Art Moran stood rubbing his lip and stared hard at Horace Whaley. 'That bang to the head,' he said. 'That bang to the head is sort of . . . funny, you know?'

Horace Whaley nodded. 'Could be,' he said.

'Couldn't it be that somebody hit him?' asked the sheriff. 'Isn't that a possibility?'

'You want to play Sherlock Holmes?' asked Horace. 'You going to play detective?'

'Not really. But Sherlock Holmes isn't here, is he? And this wound in Carl's head is.'

'That's true,' said Horace. 'You got that part right.'

Then – and afterwards he would remember this; during the trial of Kabuo Miyamoto, Horace Whaley would recall having spoken these words (though he would not repeat them in the witness box) – he said to Art Moran that if he wanted to play Sherlock Holmes he ought to start looking for a Jap with a bloody gun handle – a right-handed Jap, to be precise.

◆

Once Horace Whaley had finished giving his account to the prosecuting counsel, Nels Gudmundsson rose a second time.

'Horace,' he said. 'Good morning.'

'Morning, Nels,' answered the coroner.

'You've said quite a bit,' Nels Gudmundsson reminded him. 'You've told the court in detail about your examination of the deceased, your fine background as a medical examiner, as you've been asked to do. And, well, I'm troubled by a couple of matters.'

'Go ahead,' urged Horace Whaley.

Nels Gudmundsson started to work through Horace Whaley's report point by point. He considered the blood and air mixture in Carl Heine's lungs, how it had to be formed by the action of a man drowning, not by water entering a dead man's lungs. He questioned him about the cut on Carl Heine's hand, confirming that it had happened at a time close to when Carl Heine had died. And Nels Gudmundsson questioned Horace at length about the flat wound above Carl Heine's left ear. He asked Horace to confirm that there was nothing to show that this had not been caused by falling against the side of the boat or any other piece of equipment. That, in short, nothing showed for certain that Carl Heine had been the victim of an attack. There was no proof that it had been murder, and Horace Whaley had to agree.

◆

Art Moran, from his place in the gallery, felt a strange satisfaction watching Horace Whaley suffer. He remembered his comment: Sherlock Holmes. He remembered leaving Horace's office, waiting a moment before going up to Mill Run Road to bring the news to the dead man's wife.

Driving up to see Susan Marie Heine, Art thought out his words in silence, changing them as he went and planning how he should behave. 'Excuse me, Mrs Heine. I am sorry to report that your husband, Carl Gunther Heine, was killed last night in an accident at sea. May I . . .' But this would not do. She was not unknown to him; he couldn't treat her like a stranger. The thought of telling her about Carl's death was more than just upsetting to Art, and as he drove he struggled to find the proper words, the phrases that would free him without too much awkwardness from the message he carried to this woman. But it seemed to him there were none.

Art Moran knew that he would not go inside the house this time. He knew that suddenly. He'd stand outside. He understood that this was not right, but on the other hand what else could he do? It was just too difficult for him.

When he got to the Heines' house, he climbed to the front entrance with his hat in his hand and knocked on the door, which was thrown open to let in the summer light. While he stood waiting, she appeared at the top of the stairs.

'Sheriff Moran,' she called. 'Hello.'

He knew then that she hadn't heard the news. He knew it was his job to say it. But he couldn't just yet, couldn't make himself, and so he only stood there with his hat in his hands rubbing his lips with his thumb while she came down the stairs. 'Hello, Mrs Heine,' he said.

'I was just putting the baby to bed,' she answered.

It was a far different woman from the one at church, the wife serving tea and coffee. Now she wore a dull skirt, no shoes, and no make-up. There was a cloth over her shoulder and a baby bottle in her hand.

'What can I do for you, Sheriff?' she asked. 'Carl hasn't come home yet.'

'That's why I'm here,' Art replied. 'I'm afraid I have some . . . bad news to report. The worst sort of news, Mrs Heine.'

She seemed at first not to understand. She looked at him as if he'd spoken in Chinese.

'Carl is dead,' said Art Moran. 'He died last night in a fishing accident. We found him this morning caught in his net out in White Sand Bay.'

'Carl?' said Susan Marie Heine. 'That can't be.'

'It is, though. I know it can't be. I don't want it to be. Believe me, I wish it wasn't true. But it is true. I've come to tell you.'

It was strange, the way she reacted. There was no way to have predicted it ahead of time. Suddenly she backed away from him, sat down hard on the bottom stair, and set the baby bottle on the floor beside her toes. She dug her elbows into her stomach and began to rock with the cloth between her hands, twisting it between her fingers. 'I knew this would happen one day,' she whispered. Then she stopped rocking and stared into the living room.

'I'm sorry,' Art said. 'I'm ... I'm going to call your sister, I think, and ask her to come on over. Is that all right with you, Mrs Heine?'

Chapter 6   Japanese Americans

During the morning break the accused man's wife had asked permission to speak with her husband.

'You'll have to do it from back there,' said Abel Martinson. 'Mr Miyamoto can turn and face you all right, but that's all, you see. I'm not supposed to let him move around much.'

Kabuo turned towards Hatsue. 'How are the kids?' he said.

'They need their father,' she answered.

'Where are they staying?' asked Kabuo.

'They're at your mother's. Mrs Nakao is there. Everybody is helping out.'

'You look good. I miss you.'

'I look terrible,' answered Hatsue. 'And you look like an enemy soldier. You'd better stop sitting up so straight and tall. These jury people will be afraid of you.'

Hatsue was a woman of thirty-one and still graceful. She had the flat-footed way of walking of a peasant, a narrow waist, small breasts. She very often wore men's trousers, a grey cotton shirt, and open-toed shoes. It was her habit in the summer to work at picking strawberries in order to bring home extra money. Hatsue was a tall woman, five foot eight, but nevertheless could bend low between the strawberry rows.

When she was younger she was a great beauty, and she had been crowned princess of the Strawberry Festival in 1941. When she was thirteen her mother had made her put on traditional Japanese dress and sent her off to Mrs Shigemura, who taught young girls to dance and to serve tea. Seated before a mirror, with Mrs Shigemura behind her, she had learned that her hair was a thing of perfection and should not be cut. It was a river of shining black, said Mrs Shigemura, as she combed it down Hatsue's back. Mrs Shigemura also tried to teach her how to become calm, at peace with herself, telling her that in America there was fear of death; here life was separate from Being. A Japanese, on the other hand, must see that life is part of death, and when she feels the truth of this she will gain peace. Mrs Shigemura trained Hatsue to sit without moving, to become completely still. In this way, she said, she could become happy.

Her parents had sent Hatsue to Mrs Shigemura so that the girl would not forget that she was Japanese. Her father, a strawberry farmer, had come from Japan, from people who had been pottery makers for as long as anyone could remember. Hatsue's mother, Fujiko, was the daughter of a family near Kobe, hardworking shopkeepers and rice dealers. The marriage had been arranged by a woman the family knew. The woman had told the Shibayamas that the future husband had made a fortune in the new country, even showing a picture of the farm she would live on.

But this had not been true. There was no farm, no money, and it had taken years for Fujiko to learn to forgive her husband, and more years for them to build some sort of a life for themselves on this island.

'It's snowing hard,' Hatsue said to Kabuo, lifting her eyes to the courtroom windows. 'A big snow. Your son's first.'

He watched the snow for a silent moment, then turned again to look at her. 'Do you remember that snow at Manzanar? And the starlight coming through the window?'

It was not the sort of thing he would normally have said to her, these romantic words. But perhaps prison had taught him to show what otherwise he might hide. 'That was prison, too,' said Hatsue. 'There were good things, but that was prison.'

'It wasn't prison,' Kabuo told her. 'We thought it was back then because we didn't know any better. But it wasn't prison.' And as he spoke, she knew that this was true.

They'd been married at the camp in the Californian desert where Japanese Americans had been held during the war. Her mother had hung thick army sheets to divide the Imadas' room in half and had given them, on their wedding night, two narrow beds pushed together to form one bed and smoothed their sheets with her hands. Hatsue's sisters, all four of them, had stood beside the curtain watching while their mother went about her silent business.

They stood beside the window in their wedding clothes and kissed, and she smelled his warm neck and throat. Outside the snow had piled up against the walls. 'They'll hear everything,' Hatsue whispered.

Kabuo, his hands at her waist, turned and spoke to the curtain. 'There must be something good on the radio,' he called. 'Wouldn't some music be nice?'

They waited. Kabuo hung his coat on a hook. In a little while a radio station from Las Vegas came on – dance music. Kabuo sat down and removed his shoes and socks. He put them under the bed neatly. He unknotted his tie.

Hatsue sat down beside him. She looked at the side of his face for a moment, and then they kissed.

'I don't want to make a lot of noise,' she said. 'Even with the radio. My sisters are listening.'

'OK,' said Kabuo. 'Quietly.'

He unbuttoned his shirt, took it off, and set it on the end of the bed. He pulled his undershirt off. He was strong and muscular. She was glad to have married him. She kissed his jaw and forehead more softly, and then she put her chin against the top of his head and held his ears between her fingers. His hair smelled like wet earth. Kabuo put his hands against her back and pulled her to him.

'You smell so good,' he said.

She remembered how she had kissed Ishmael Chambers, her childhood boyfriend. He was a brown-skinned boy who lived down the road. They'd picked blackberries, climbed trees, fished together. She thought of him while Kabuo kissed her, and she recognized Ishmael as the beginning of a chain, that she had kissed a boy when she was fourteen years old, had even then felt something strange, and that tonight, soon, she would be in another boy's arms.

She could see Kabuo's face in the starlight from the window now. It was a good face, strong and smooth. The wind was blowing hard outside now, and the sound of it whistled between the boards. She held him tightly.

'Have you ever done this before?' he whispered.

'Never,' answered Hatsue. 'You're the only one.' Then she whispered, 'It's right. It feels so right, Kabuo.'

'*Tadaima aware ga wakatta*,' he had answered. 'I understand just now the deepest beauty.'

Eight days later he left for Camp Shelby, Mississippi, where he joined the 442nd Army Group. He had to go to the war, he told her. It was necessary in order to demonstrate his bravery. It was necessary to demonstrate his loyalty to the United States: his country. It was not only a point of honour, he'd said, it was also a matter of having to go because his face was Japanese. There was something extra that had to be proved.

Hatsue settled into missing her husband and learned the art of waiting, a deliberately controlled fear that was something like what Ishmael Chambers felt watching her in the courtroom.

Chapter 7   The Beach and the Woods

Ishmael Chambers, watching Hatsue, remembered digging for shellfish with her at South Beach. They had spent the summer working together like this, finding the big shellfish that lived in the mud, taking turns digging them out. They were fourteen years old; it was summer and little else really mattered. When they were not digging in the mud they would float in the warm water side by side, looking through his glass-bottomed box at the shellfish and the sea plants.

The 14-year-old Ishmael had been unhappy when he thought about her lately, and he had passed a lot of time, all spring long, thinking how to tell her about his unhappiness. Although they had been secret friends since they began school, they had also remained strangers in public. It had to be that way because she was Japanese and he wasn't. It was the way things were and there was nothing to be done about such a basic thing.

As they floated in the water, looking through the glass-bottomed box, he had said, 'I like you. Do you know what I mean? I've always liked you, Hatsue.'

She didn't answer. She didn't even look at him; she looked down. But having started it he moved into the warmth of her face anyway and put his lips against hers. They were warm, too. There was the taste of salt and the heat of her breathing. She pushed back against him, and he felt the pressure of her teeth and smelled the inside of her mouth.

As soon as they were no longer touching, she jumped up and

ran away down the beach. She was very fast, he knew that. He stood up only to watch her go. Then, after she had disappeared into the woods, he lay in the water for another ten minutes feeling the kiss many times. He decided then that he would love her for ever, no matter what happened.

A week after this kiss, at the start of the strawberry season, Ishmael saw Hatsue on the South Beach wood path underneath silent cedars. They were both of them going to work for Mr Nitta, who paid better than any berry farmer on the island, for thirty-five cents a basket.

He walked behind her, his lunch in hand. He caught up and said hello. Neither said anything about their kiss on the beach two weeks before. They walked along the path quietly as it went towards the sea, down into a valley known as Devil's Dip, and then as it climbed among cedars and the deep shadows of the trees before going down into Center Valley.

They did not pick berries together, but Ishmael, from three rows away, watched Hatsue at her work. Her hair soon came loose from its arrangement. She picked quickly and filled two baskets in the time it took other pickers to fill one and a half. She was among friends, a half-dozen Japanese girls working in the rows together, their faces hidden by sun hats, and she would not show that she knew him when he passed her.

Late in the afternoon, when rain had forced them out of the strawberry fields, Ishmael saw Hatsue cross the Nittas' upper fields and go into the cedar woods, walking south. He found himself following – the rain was warm and felt good on his face – through the woods towards a hollow tree they'd played in together when they were only nine years old.

Ishmael sat beneath it in the rain and for half a minute watched the place where you could enter the tree. His hair hung wet in his eyes. He tried to understand what had brought her here; he himself had forgotten about the place, which was a good half-mile from his home. He remembered, now, how it was possible to kneel but not to stand, though on the other hand the room inside the tree was wide enough to lie down in. Then he saw that Hatsue was looking at him from the entrance to the hollow cedar tree. He looked back; there was no point in hiding.

'You'd better come in,' she said. 'It's still raining.'

'All right,' he answered.

Inside the tree he knelt on the leaves with water dripping beneath his shirt. Hatsue sat there, too, in her wet summer dress, her hat beside her. 'You followed me,' she said. 'Didn't you?'

'I didn't mean to,' Ishmael apologized. 'It just happened, sort of. I was going home. Sorry,' he added. 'I followed you.'

She smoothed her hair back behind her ears. 'I'm all wet,' she said.

'So am I. It feels good, sort of. Anyway it's dry in here. Remember this place? It seems smaller.'

'I've been coming here all the time,' said Hatsue. 'I come here to think. Nobody else comes around. I haven't seen anybody here in years.'

Ishmael lay down with his hands supporting his chin and looked out at the rain. The inside of the tree felt private. He felt they would never be discovered here. It was surprising how much light entered from the cedar forest.

'I'm sorry I kissed you on the beach,' said Ishmael. 'Let's just forget about it. Forget it happened.'

There was no answer at first. It was like Hatsue not to answer. He himself was always in need of words, even when he couldn't quite find them, but she seemed capable of a kind of silence he couldn't feel inside.

She picked up her hat and looked at it instead of him. 'Don't be sorry,' she said with her eyes down. 'I'm not sorry about it.'

'Nor am I,' said Ishmael.

She lay down on her back beside him. The green light caught

her face. He wanted to put his mouth against hers and leave it there for ever. He knew now that he might do so without being made to feel sorry afterwards. 'Do you think this is wrong?' she asked.

'Other people do,' said Ishmael. 'Your friends would,' he added. 'And your parents.'

'So would yours,' said Hatsue. 'So would your mother and father.'

'Yours more than mine,' said Ishmael. 'If they knew we were out here in this tree together . . .' He shook his head and laughed softly. 'Your father'd probably kill me. He'd cut me into little pieces.'

'Probably not,' said Hatsue. 'But you're right, he would be angry. With both of us, for doing this.'

'But what are we doing? We're talking.'

'Still,' said Hatsue, 'you're not Japanese. And I'm alone with you.'

'It doesn't matter,' answered Ishmael.

They lay beside each other in the cedar tree talking until half an hour had gone by. Then, once again, they kissed. They felt comfortable kissing inside the tree, and they kissed for another half-hour. With the rain falling outside and the leaves soft under him, Ishmael shut his eyes and breathed the smell of her fully. He told himself he had never felt so happy, and he felt a sort of ache that this was happening and would never again happen in just this way no matter how long he lived.

Chapter 8   Etta Heine

And now Ishmael was sitting in the courtroom where Hatsue's husband was on trial for murder. He found he was watching her as she spoke to Kabuo, and he made himself look away.

The jurors returned, and then Judge Fielding, and Carl Heine's mother, Etta, a widow of German background like her husband, went into the witness box. She had come to the States in her childhood and still spoke English with a strong accent. Alvin Hooks, the prosecutor, first asked Mrs Heine about the strawberry farm she had lived on until 1944, her reasons for selling when her husband died, and her present finances. He seemed particularly interested in the money, and questioned her for nearly an hour on the subject, building a picture of careful management and domestic economy. He then moved on to the subject of Kabuo Miyamoto.

Yes, she'd known the defendant, Kabuo Miyamoto, and his family, for a good long time. She remembered them well. How was she supposed to forget such people? She could remember how Zenhichi Miyamoto had appeared at her door at the end of his family's third picking season, asking to speak to Carl, her husband. How Carl had agreed to sell seven acres of land – sell it for a cash deposit and two hundred and fifty dollars twice a year for the next eight years.

The arrangement, she explained to Alvin Hooks, included a five-hundred-dollar deposit and an eight-year 'lease to own' contract. The Miyamotos – this was back in '34, said Etta – couldn't really own land anyway. They were from Japan, both of them born there, and there was this law on the books that prevented them.

'One moment,' Judge Fielding interrupted. 'Excuse me for interrupting, Mrs Heine. The court has a few things to say about these matters. Pardon me for interrupting.'

'All right,' said Etta.

Judge Fielding nodded at her, then turned his attention towards the jury. 'I'm going to have to interrupt the witness in order to explain a point of law.'

He rubbed his eyes, then drank some water. He put down his

glass and began again. 'The witness makes reference to a previous law of the State of Washington which made it illegal at the time of which she speaks for a non-citizen to own land. This same law also stated that no person shall hold land for a non-citizen in any way, shape, or form. Mrs Heine has told us that her deceased husband made an illegal agreement with the defendant's deceased father to find a way around this law. The witness's husband and the defendant's father entered into a so-called 'lease' agreement that hid an actual purchase. However, as the people who entered this agreement are no longer among us, this matter is not an issue for this court. If counsel or witness feel any more explanation is required, they may inquire further,' the judge added. 'Mr Hooks, you may proceed.'

Alvin Hooks nodded and paced again. 'Mrs Heine,' he said, 'let's go back just a moment. If the law, as you say, prevented the Miyamotos from owning land, what was the point of this sale agreement?'

'So they could make payments,' said Etta. 'The law let 'em own land if they were citizens. Them Miyamoto kids were born here so they're citizens, I guess. When they turned twenty the land would go over into their name – law said they could do that, put it in their kid's name at twenty. It'd go to the oldest one sitting right there,' said Etta, pointing a finger at Kabuo. 'He was twelve, I believe, back then. November of '42 he'd be twenty, they'd make the last payment December 31st, the land would go over into his name, that was going to be that.'

'Going to be?' said Alvin Hooks.

'Missed the last payment,' said Etta. 'Missed the last two payments, in fact. Never made 'em. The last two. Out of sixteen total.' She folded her arms across her chest. She set her mouth and waited.

'Now Mrs Heine,' said Hooks, 'when they missed two payments in 1942, what did you do about that?'

It took her a while to answer. She remembered how Carl senior had come home one afternoon to tell her that all the Japanese on San Piedro and the other islands were to be removed for the rest of the war, and how Zenhichi Miyamoto came to the door to talk things over with him. How Zenhichi Miyamoto stood there nodding – it was how they got the better of you, they acted small, thought big, said nothing, kept their faces turned down was how they got things like her seven acres. Said he wanted to give one hundred and twenty dollars immediately, but Carl senior would not take his savings when he had so many other problems. Said that they would sort things out, that there was no need to worry. They could sort things out after the war.

But then Carl senior died and the Miyamotos still hadn't made their final payments, she told Alvin Hooks. Simple as that. Didn't make them. So she sold the place off to Ole Jurgensen, sent their money on down to them in California, didn't try to hold back their money. Gave every penny back. She moved into Amity Harbor Christmastime '44. That was that, she'd thought. Looked, now, like she was wrong about one thing: you were never finished with people where money or land was concerned. One way or another. And on account of that, she told the court, her son had been murdered by Kabuo Miyamoto. Her son was dead and gone.

Chapter 9   Transactions

'Did you hear again from the Miyamotos after that? After you sent them their money?' Alvin Hooks asked Etta Heine.

'I heard from them,' said Etta.

'When was that?' Alvin Hooks asked.

Etta bit her lip and told how Kabuo Miyamoto had come to her door when he came back from the army, and how he had accused her of stealing his family's land.

'And what did you say to that?' asked Alvin Hooks.

'I told him that Carl senior had died, and Carl junior was still fighting the Japs. Told him I'd done nothing illegal. They'd never made their payments. Two payments down. I'd done no more than the bank would.'

'Mrs Heine,' said the prosecutor, Alvin Hooks, when she'd finished telling of these things. 'Did you see the defendant after this? Did he approach you again about these land matters?'

'Small town, of course I saw him – but I never saw a friendly look from him, not once in all the times I saw him. Always narrowin' his eyes at me, giving me mean looks.'

'Mrs Heine,' said Alvin Hooks. 'Did you tell Carl junior that Kabuo Miyamoto had come to your door and argued with you about the sale of your family's land?'

'My son knew all about it. I told him about the dirty looks and he said he'd watch out for him.'

'He watched out for Kabuo Miyamoto?'

'Yes, he did. He did that.'

'Mrs Heine,' said Alvin Hooks. 'Do you think that the term "enemy" could be accurately applied to the relationship between your son and the defendant? Were they enemies?'

Etta looked directly at Kabuo. 'Yes,' she said. 'We're enemies all right. They've been bothering us over those seven acres for near ten years now. My son was killed over it.'

'Thank you,' Alvin Hooks said. 'But I can't think of anything else I want to ask, Your Honour. Mrs Heine, I want you to know that I appreciate your coming down, though, in this terrible weather we've been having.' He turned, now, on the toe of one shoe; he pointed a finger at Nels Gudmundsson. 'Your witness,' he said.

Nels Gudmundsson shook his head. 'Just three questions,' he said, without getting up. 'I've done some calculating, Mrs Heine. If I've multiplied correctly, the Miyamoto family purchased seven acres from you for forty-five hundred dollars, is that right?'

'Tried to buy it for that much,' said Etta. 'Never finished their payments.'

'Second question,' Nels said. 'When you went to Ole Jurgensen in 1944 and told him you wanted to sell him your land, what was the price per acre?'

'A thousand,' said Etta. 'Thousand per acre.'

'I guess that makes what would have been forty-five hundred dollars into seven thousand dollars instead, doesn't it. A twenty-five hundred dollar increase in the land's value if you sent the Miyamotos their money and sold the land to Ole Jurgensen?'

'Is that your third question?' said Etta.

'It is,' said Nels. 'Yes.'

'You done your calculations right. Twenty-five hundred.'

'That's all then, thank you, Mrs Heine,' Nels replied.

◆

Ole Jurgensen was the next witness, now a very old man. He told the court how he had bought the Heine farm when Carl senior died – and how Kabuo Miyamoto had come to see him when he came back from the war. Ole told him to take his problem to Etta Heine – he had bought the land legally and he felt there was nothing else he could do. Then illness had made him sell his farm – including the Heine land – and he had sold it to Carl Heine. He'd advertised it just one day and Carl had come the next wanting to buy the farm, saying he wanted to stop fishing and go back on the land. They'd shaken hands there and then, Ole saying he could wait for the money until Carl had sold his boat.

'Did anyone else come looking to buy the land?' asked Nels.

'Kabuo Miyamoto came. The same day Carl Heine came to see me. Said he wanted to buy the land. We had to say we was sorry but it was already sold.'

'Did he ask who had bought it?'

'Sure, we told him Carl Heine had.'

'How did he take that?'

'Didn't say much. Didn't look happy about it. Said maybe he'd talk to Carl.'

Chapter 10   Kabuo Miyamoto

In his cell beneath the courthouse, Kabuo Miyamoto looked at his face in a small mirror. His wife had said he looked like an enemy soldier. He wanted to see if this was so. He could see how his face had once been a boy's face and how on top of this was laid the face of his war years, a face he was no longer surprised to see. He had come home from the war and seen in his own eyes the empty spaces he'd seen in the eyes of other soldiers he'd known.

Kabuo remembered how he had shot the young German soldier in the woods above Monte Casino.* As Kabuo approached him, the boy had stared up at him and spoken in frightened German. Then the boy moved his hand toward his gun, and Kabuo shot him one more time in the heart. When the boy spoke again it was clear to Kabuo that he wanted the American who had killed him to save him – he had no choice but to ask him for this, nobody else was present. And then the boy stopped talking and blood ran from his mouth and down his cheeks.

Kabuo sat in his prison cell now and examined his reflection carefully. It was not a thing he had control over. His face had been shaped by his experiences as a soldier, and if he seemed to be locked up inside it was because this was how he felt. What could

---

* Monte Casino: a place in Italy where there was an important battle during the Second World War.

he do about it? And yes, he was able to see how Hatsue might see him, how the men and women on the jury might have seen him. In his attempt to appear as open as possible, to show his soul to the jury, he now understood that he had only appeared cold and proud. The face in the hand mirror was none other than the face he had worn since the war. He felt himself to be guilty of murder, to have murdered men in the course of war, and it was this that lived in him always and that he tried not to communicate.

Sitting in his cell now, he realized how much he missed Hatsue and his children. Then he remembered his wife before she'd married him, her long hair tied back as she moved from her family's house to the vegetable garden next to the strawberry fields. He also saw her just as he had seen her in history class, a pencil between her teeth, one hand laid against the back of her neck, lost behind her hair. She walked through the corridors with her books pressed against her breasts, in a cotton skirt and blouse, white socks folded down above the polished black tops of her shoes. She looked at him and then away again quickly, saying nothing when he passed by.

He remembered the camp for Japanese Americans at Manzanar, the dust in the army huts, in the paper-walled rooms; even the bread tasted of sand. They'd worked in the camp garden. They'd been paid little, the hours were long, they'd been told it was their duty to work hard. He and Hatsue spoke of little things at first, then of the San Piedro fields they'd left behind and the smell of strawberries. He had begun to love her, to love more than just her beauty and grace, and when he saw that in their hearts they shared the same dream he felt a great certainty about her. They kissed in the back of a lorry coming into camp one night, and the warm wet taste of her, however brief, brought her down for him from heaven into the world of human beings. In this way his love deepened.

He remembered the look on Hatsue's face when he told her

he had joined the army. Hatsue said that she accepted he would have to do what he must do, and she would have to do the same, but he could see that he had hurt her. He'd nodded and tried to show nothing. Then he turned and had walked twenty yards when she called his name and asked if he would marry her before leaving. 'Why do you want to marry me?' he asked, and her answer came back, 'To hold a part of you.' She walked the twenty yards to hold him in her arms 'It's my character, too,' she whispered. 'I must love you now.'

He remembered, too, his father's face, and the sword his father kept inside a wooden chest in the days before Pearl Harbor.[*] It had been in the Miyamoto family, it was said, for six centuries. An undecorated and highly useful weapon, its beauty lay in its simplicity, the plainness of its curve.

Kabuo's training in *kendo* had begun when he was seven. His father had taken him one Saturday to the community centre hall. While he sat on his heels, his father explained softly that a soldier must understand that the world is full of danger, a danger that is always waiting to catch those who are not prepared. Then he took down a wooden stick from the wall and, before Kabuo knew what had happened, hit him with it in the stomach.

'There is always danger!' said Zenhichi, while the boy caught his breath. 'Didn't you say you understood?'

The first time he held a weapon was in the strawberry fields early one July morning just after the picking season was finished. The practice stick, a curved piece of wood three feet long, had belonged to Kabuo's great-grandfather, a man who had been a *samurai*[†] at the beginning of the nineteenth century and later,

---

[*] Pearl Harbor: the US harbour on the island of Hawaii which was attacked by the Japanese airforce on 7th December, 1941. This attack brought the USA into the Second World War in Asia.

[†] samurai: the samurai were the traditional fighting class in Japan until major changes in the social system were introduced in 1871.

after the wearing of swords was made illegal, had been killed fighting the government army, believing that swords could be used to beat guns.

From that day Kabuo worked regularly with his father, learning the cut that will split a man's head from top to bottom, leaving one eye on each side of the nose, the skull in two parts; the four strokes, from left and right, upward and downward, that can remove an arm; the stroke that swings in from the left and which can take a man's legs from under him; and, finally, the most common of *kendo* strokes, a blow which a right-handed man can strike with great force against the left side of his enemy's head.

By the time he was sixteen there was no longer anyone at the community centre who could defeat him, not even the half-dozen grown men on the island for whom *kendo* was a serious hobby – not even his father, who acknowledged his son's success without shame, although he feared for his son's willingness to draw on his dark side in order to achieve a final victory.

It was only after he'd killed four Germans that Kabuo saw how right his father had been. This dark anger had been passed down in the blood of the Miyamoto family and he himself had to carry it into the next generation. The story of his great-grandfather, the *samurai* madman, was his own story, too, he saw now.

Sitting where he sat now, accused of the murder of Carl Heine, it seemed to him he'd found the place of suffering he had desired. For Kabuo Miyamoto felt it was now his duty to pay for the lives he had taken in anger.

Chapter 11   Lies

Outside the wind blew steadily from the north, driving snow against the courthouse. By midday three inches had settled on the town like the breath of spirits, up and down Amity Harbor's streets – powdery dust devils, twists of white smoke. Ishmael Chambers was out walking aimlessly in the snow, admiring it and remembering. The trial of Kabuo Miyamoto had brought that world back for him.

He remembered the many times, over four years, when he and Hatsue had held one another with the dreamy contentedness of young lovers. The cedar tree had been a secret home, somewhere where they could lie down fully-clothed and touch each other – the heat of it and the cedar smell, the rain outside, the slippery softness of their lips and tongues made them feel as if the world had disappeared; there was nobody and nothing but the two of them.

Ishmael, at school, pretended to have no special relationship with her, ignoring her in the way she gradually taught him to use. At the Strawberry Festival in 1941 he'd watched while the leader of Amity Harbor Council had crowned Hatsue Strawberry Princess and Ishmael's father, owner, editor, chief reporter, photographer and printer of the *San Piedro Review*, had taken the photographs for the 'special' he would write tomorrow.

'Neighbour girl,' his father said. 'South Beach ought to be proud.'

Hatsue told him, one autumn afternoon, about her training with Mrs Shigemura and the instruction she'd been given as a girl of thirteen to marry a boy of her own kind, a Japanese boy from a good family. She repeated that it made her unhappy to deceive the world. Her secret life, which she carried with her in the presence of her parents and sisters at every moment, made her feel nothing less than evil – there was no other word for it, she told Ishmael. Outside, the rain dripped from the roof of cedar branches down into the undergrowth. Hatsue sat with her cheek against her knees, looking out through the opening in the cedar tree, her hair like a single silken rope down her back. 'It isn't evil,' Ishmael insisted. 'How can this be evil? It wouldn't make any sense for this to be evil. It's the world that's evil, Hatsue,' he added. 'Don't worry about it.'

Later they lay side by side, looking up into the darkened cedar wood with their hands folded behind their heads.

'This can't go on,' whispered Hatsue. 'Don't you worry about that?'

'I know,' answered Ishmael. 'You're right.'

'What will we do? What's the answer?'

'I don't know,' said Ishmael. 'There isn't one, it looks like.'

Chapter 12   Pearl Harbor

And then the Japanese airforce had bombed Pearl Harbor. The attack which brought the United States into the Second World War also seemed to give an excuse to many of the islanders to express the mistrust and dislike they felt for their Japanese neighbours.

Hatsue Imada and members of other Japanese families listened to the news on a radio in one of the local stores. Nobody spoke – they listened for ten minutes without moving, their heads down, their ears turned toward the radio. When the news programme was over, Hatsue's father turned and looked at her for what seemed like a long time. 'We'd better get home,' he said.

During the day armed men had positioned themselves around Amity Harbor out of fear of a Japanese attack. There were men with guns behind trees along the beach just north and south of town. The defence of San Piedro was being organized.

At school, all day, there was nothing but the radio. Two thousand men had been killed. By three o'clock that afternoon Ishmael's father had printed the first 'war extra' in the history of his island newspaper, a one-page edition with the headline, ISLAND DEFENCE IS READY! – and an account of the preparations that were being made in case there was an attack from the air or the sea.

Ishmael sat reading his father's words in the cedar tree; he was rereading them when Hatsue came in and sat down beside him. 'My father was up all night writing this paper.' said Ishmael.

'My father can't get our money from the bank,' Hatsue replied. 'We have a few dollars, and the rest we can't get. My parents aren't citizens.'

'What will you do?'

'We don't know.'

'I have twenty dollars from the picking season,' said Ishmael. 'You can have all of it, you can just have it. I'll bring it to school in the morning.'

'No,' said Hatsue. 'Don't bring it. I could never accept your money.'

Ishmael turned onto his side, towards her, and supported himself on his elbow. 'It's hard to believe,' he said.

'It's so unreal,' answered Hatsue. 'It just isn't fair, it's not fair. How could they do this, just like that? How did we get ourselves into this?'

'We didn't get ourselves into it,' said Ishmael. 'The Japanese forced us into it. And on a Sunday morning, when no one was ready. It's cheap, if you ask me. They—'

'Look at my face,' interrupted Hatsue. 'Look at my eyes, Ishmael. My face is the face of the people who did it, don't you see what I mean? My face, it's how the Japanese look. My parents came to San Piedro from Japan. My mother and father, they hardly speak English. My family is in bad trouble now. Do you see what I mean? We're going to have trouble.'

'Wait a minute,' said Ishmael. 'You're not Japanese. You're—'

'You heard the news. They're arresting people. How can this be happening?' she added. 'How did things get like this?'

They crossed the small stream below their tree and followed

the path down the hillside. It was early evening and the sea wind blew in their faces. Standing in the path with their arms around each other they kissed once and then again, the second time with greater force. 'Don't let this hurt us,' Ishmael said. 'I don't care about what's happening in the world. We're not going to let this hurt us.'

'It won't,' said Hatsue. 'You'll see.'

During the next weeks, although there was no attack, things did get worse for the Japanese community. They found they could no longer travel from the island to Seattle or Anacortes, found that they were moved from their homes if they were near military positions. Ishmael's father continued to write his newspaper, giving information from the government about the defence of the island and trying to keep a balance of opinions on the position of the Japanese Americans on the island. He used gentle good humour to stop violence breaking out after explosives were found at a Japanese home – all the farmers on the island used them when clearing dead trees. His attempt at balance was not appreciated by all.

'Seems like you're favouring the Japs, Art,' wrote someone who did not give their name. 'You're putting them on the front page every week and writing all about their loyalty to America. Well maybe it's time you pulled your head from the sand and realized there's a war on! And whose side are you on, anyway?' In January, fifteen islanders cancelled their orders for the paper. One of them, Herbert Langlie, wrote: 'Your newspaper is an insult to all white Americans. Please cancel my order for your paper as of this date.'

Two weeks later, on 4th February, a black Ford came through the Imadas' fields, making for the house of cedar wood. Two men got out of it in suits and ties. They shut their doors gently and looked at each other; one of them straightened his jacket a little – he was bigger than the other, and his sleeves were not long enough.

They were FBI* agents, come to make a search of the house – a neighbour had said that Hatsue's father owned a gun. The agents searched the house and found Hisao's shotgun and an old sword. In the storeroom at the back of the house they also found a box of explosives. Although Hisao explained that it was only for clearing land, they told him he should have handed it in six weeks earlier. They would have to arrest him.

Robert Nishi had been arrested as well. Ronald Kobayashi, Richard Sumida, Saburo Oda, Taro Kato, Junkoh Kitano, Kenzi Yamamoto, John Masui, Robert Nishi, they were all in a Seattle prison now. They had all been arrested on the same night.

After this night of arrests, stories started to circulate that all the Japanese on the coast were going to be forced to leave. Hatsue's mother tried to prepare her daughters by explaining that in Japan a person learned not to complain or be worried about suffering. It was best to accept old age, death, injustice – all of these were part of living. Only a foolish girl would deny this was so. To deny that there was this dark side to life would be like pretending that the cold of winter was not real.

'Do you understand?' she said in Japanese. 'There is no choice in the matter. We will all have to suffer and accept.'

'They don't all hate us,' Hatsue replied. 'They're not so different from us. Some hate, others don't. It isn't all of them.'

Fujiko said, in Japanese. 'You sound very certain, oldest daughter. The words fly from your mouth. Is this what you think when you walk by yourself in the woods each day? I hope you know yourself as well as you seem to. I am not so sure of myself, oldest daughter. Sometimes to be so sure means that you have lost yourself. I hope that this is not so, more for you than for me in these difficult times.'

---

* FBI: the Federal Bureau of Investigation is the national organization in the US which is responsible for investigating serious crime.

Hatsue found herself walking in the woods later that afternoon. She went away from the sea to where the cedars stopped growing. Everything was familiar and known to her here – the dead and dying cedars, the fallen, defeated trees as high as a house, the upturned roots, the low wet places. Deep among the trees she lay on a fallen log and looked up at the branchless trunks. A late winter wind blew the tops around. The world was impossibly complicated, and yet this forest made a simple sense in her heart that she felt nowhere else.

Lying on the fallen log she thought she understood what she had long tried to understand, that she hid her love for Ishmael Chambers not because she was Japanese in her heart but because what she felt for him was not love at all. Knowing this, and now knowing that her mother had seen the trouble in her heart, she also knew that she had to find some way of cutting through all these knots, of returning to herself.

The problem of how to solve these problems was taken out of her hands, when on 21st March the US Government announced that Japanese Americans on the island had eight days to prepare to leave.

On Sunday afternoon, at four o'clock, Hatsue told her mother she was going for a walk. She wanted to sit in the forest, she said, and think about matters for a while. Ishmael, she found, was waiting for her at the hollow tree. 'This is it,' she said to him. 'Tomorrow morning we leave.'

They lay down, not touching, in silence, Hatsue with her hair over one shoulder now, Ishmael with his hands on his knees. The March wind came up outside the tree and they heard it joined with the sound of the water in the little stream just below. The tree softened these sounds, and Hatsue felt herself at the heart of things. This place, this tree, was safe.

They began to kiss, but the emptiness she felt filled everything and she found she couldn't put her thoughts away. She placed a finger against Ishmael's lips and shut her eyes and let her hair fall back. The smell of the tree was his smell, too, and the smell of the place she was leaving the next day, and she began to understand how she would miss it. The ache of it filled her; she felt sorry for him and sorry for herself and began to cry so quietly that it was only behind her eyes, a tightness in her throat. Hatsue pressed against him, crying in this silent way, and breathed in the smell of Ishmael's throat.

'Let's get married,' he said, and she understood what he meant. 'I just . . . I want to marry you.'

She made no move to stop him when he touched her. 'Just say yes,' he whispered. 'Say yes, oh God, say yes.'

'Ishmael,' she whispered, and as he pushed himself closer to her, Hatsue knew that nothing about it was right. It came as an enormous shock to her, this knowledge, and at the same time it was something she had always known, something until now hidden. She pulled away from him. 'NO,' she said. 'No, Ishmael. No, Ishmael. Never.'

He pulled himself away. She put her coat on and then, sitting up, began to brush the leaves from her hair. 'I'm sorry,' she said. 'It wasn't right.'

'It seemed right to me,' answered Ishmael. 'It seemed like getting married, like being married, like you and me were married. Like the only kind of wedding we could ever have.'

'I'm sorry,' said Hatsue, picking leaves from her hair. 'I don't want you to be unhappy.'

'I *am* unhappy. You're leaving tomorrow morning.'

'I am unhappy, too,' said Hatsue. 'I'm sick with unhappiness, I feel worse than I've ever felt. I don't know anything any more.'

He walked her home, to the edge of her fields, where they separated. He stood for a moment beside a cedar tree. It was nearly evening and a March stillness held everything. Twelve years later she would still see him this way, standing at the edge of the strawberry fields beneath the cover of the silent cedars, a good-looking boy with one arm held out, as if asking her to come back.

Chapter 13   The Prison Camp

The Japanese population of San Piedro travelled slowly and uncomfortably to the prison camp in California. After the boat journey, the women and children were forced onto the empty railway coaches they would be sharing for the next week or more. For Hatsue's mother this journey was like going down into hell. They travelled for endless days and nights, with babies crying and a growing bad smell from the single toilet, until they reached a place called Mojave in the middle of an endless, still desert. They were then pushed on to buses at 8.30 in the morning, and the buses took them north over dusty roads for four hours to a place called Manzanar. Here conditions were little better. They were given huts with paper walls to live in and twelve horribly dirty toilets, in six back-to-back pairs for over three hundred people.

The Japanese people in the camp came from all over the west coast. They had nowhere to put any clothing so they lived out of their cases. The floor was cold beneath their feet, and they wore their dusty shoes until bedtime. By the end of the first week Fujiko had lost track of where her daughters were in the camp. Everybody had begun to look alike, dressed in the same War Department clothing. Only her two youngest ate with her; the other three went off with groups of young people and ate at other tables. Fujiko became silent about everything, lost in her own thoughts. All she could do was to wait for a letter from Hisao to come, but a different letter came instead.

When Hatsue's sister saw the envelope with Ishmael's false return address – Journalism Class, San Piedro High School – she could not help opening it. This mail was word from home – but it was not the kind of news she had expected:

April 4th, 1942

My Love,

I still go to our cedar tree in the afternoons every day. I shut my eyes, waiting. I dream of you and I ache for you to come home. Every moment I think of you and want to hold you. Missing you is killing me. It's like a part of me has gone away.

I'm lonely and think of you always and hope you will write to me soon. Remember to use Kenny Yamashita's name for a return address on the envelope so my parents won't suspect.

Everything here is horrible and sad and life is not worth living.

I can only hope that you find some happiness during the time we have to be apart – some happiness of some kind, Hatsue. Myself, I can only be unhappy until you are in my arms again. I can't live without you, I know that now. After all these years that we've been together, I find you're a part of me. Without you, I have nothing.

All my love forever,

ISHMAEL.

After a half-hour of walking and thinking and of reading Ishmael's letter four more times, she took it to her mother. 'Here,' she said. 'I feel bad. But I have to show this to you.'

Hatsue's mother read Ishmael Chambers's letter with a sense of disbelief, sorrow and anger. She knew that her daughter had made a great mistake and she knew that it was her duty to help her correct that mistake – but it would be hard to do. When she thought of her own marriage and how hard she had worked to make herself love Hisao after the way she had been tricked into marrying him, she felt more angry than sad. This bad thing must stop.

And yet this anger became mixed with the general sadness that had been growing in her steadily since the bombing of Pearl Harbor; it was one of the rare times in Fujiko's adult life when she felt that nothing could comfort her. She also knew that she had a duty to carry out and she told herself she would have a talk with Hatsue when the girl came back from wandering around the camp. She would put an end to this business.

When Hatsue came home, she handed Hatsue the letter. 'Here,' she said coldly. 'Your mail. I don't know how you could have been so dishonest. I will never understand it, Hatsue. You will not write again to this boy or accept his letters.'

The girl sat with the letter in her hand, tears in her eyes. 'I'm sorry,' Hatsue said. 'Forgive me, Mother. I've been dishonest with you and with myself and I've always known it.'

'And what will you do?' asked her mother.

Hatsue told her mother how she had thought about what had happened all through the journey to Manzanar and she had come to see that it had been a wrong thing to do, that she was hurting herself, her family and Ishmael by letting the relationship continue. She told her mother that she would write to Ishmael and say he must not contact her again. Their relationship was over.

'Write your own letter,' her mother said in Japanese. 'Tell him the truth about things. Put all of this in your history. Tell him the truth so you can move forward. Put this boy away now.'

The letter was written, and Fujiko took it to the post office and paid for the stamp. She then closed the envelope herself and, because the idea took hold of her suddenly, she pressed the stamp on upside-down before putting the letter in the mailbox.

It was during the months that followed that Hatsue began to notice Kabuo Miyamoto. He had already helped her mother in many ways by fixing things in the hut and making shelves and chairs for the family, and she had seen that he was kind, that he carried a peacefulness inside himself that she felt she needed.

One day she spoke to Kabuo in the hall where they had lunch and sat beside him to eat. He spoke softly to her, asked her about her dreams, and when she said she wanted an island strawberry farm he said he wanted the same thing precisely, and told her about how his family's seven acres would soon be his. When the war was over he planned to farm strawberries back home on San Piedro Island.

When she kissed him for the first time, some weeks later, she felt the sadness that was still in her, and she felt how different his mouth was from Ishmael's. She found she couldn't move within the circle of his arms and struggled against him, breathless. 'You'll have to be more gentle,' she'd whispered. 'I'll try,' Kabuo had answered.

Chapter 14   Tarawa

Ishmael Chambers trained with 750 other new soldiers at Fort Benning, Georgia, in the late summer of 1942, and was then sent to the North Island of New Zealand with the American army. There they trained without a break for weeks at Hawkes Bay. Men died during these beach landing exercises and Ishmael had never been worked so hard in his life, but through all this time he felt a strange distance from everybody. Something was dead inside him and he was uninterested in drinking and other people, and the more drunk he became the clearer his mind was and the colder he felt towards everyone.

After these weeks of training, Ishmael's unit left New Zealand and they were told that they were moving towards Tarawa in the Philippines. An officer told them that the guns on the US ships would destroy all the Japanese defences, and that they would be able to walk onto the island without a fight.

On the night of the landing a quarter-moon rose over the sea while they waited seven miles off the island of Betio, part of the Tarawa group. Ishmael ate a meal with other soldiers and, like these others, began to write a last letter. His problem was that he could not write to Hatsue about love. At this moment before battle he hated the world, and because she was part of the world he hated her with everything in his heart. He wrote, and it felt good to him to write it in just that way, 'I hate you with all my heart. I hate you, Hatsue, I hate you always.' But as soon as he had written this, he tore the sheet from his writing pad and threw it into the sea. He watched it floating on the water for a few seconds, then threw his pad in after it.

The landing on Betio was a disaster. As his boat moved in towards the coast, a whistling began to sound in Ishmael's ears, growing louder by the second. He turned to look, and at the same moment the sea behind his boat seemed to explode. The Japanese guns were still there. The American attack had not destroyed them.

For three hours they pushed toward Betio, the waves coming in over the soldiers so that nothing was dry on the small boats. The island became visible as a low black line almost on the horizon. Ishmael stood to stretch his legs now. There were fires burning all up and down Betio. Beside him two men were complaining bitterly about an Admiral Hill who was in charge of things and who had timed matters so that they were going in during daylight instead of under cover of darkness.

As they came in to the island, the noise of the guns was worse than anything he had ever heard. Ishmael had somehow arrived at the war moment little boys sometimes dream about. He was coming in from the sea, he was a radioman, and he had never been so frightened in his life.

A man named Rich Hinkle from Ureka, California, was the first among them to die as he tried to lead them onto the island.

'We'd better get out of here. Let's move it! Move! Let's go!'

'You first,' somebody answered.

Hinkle dropped down into the water. Men had begun to follow him, including Ishmael Chambers, when Hinkle was shot in the face and went down, and then the man just behind him was shot, too, and the top of his head came off. Ishmael dropped his radio and went under the water and stayed under as long as he could. When he put his head up, he saw that all the men in front of him had been hit.

He swam back behind the boat with thirty soldiers, but when it came under heavy fire the group of men who had hidden behind it began to walk towards the land. Ishmael kept to the middle of the group, swimming and keeping low, and tried to think of himself as a dead soldier floating harmlessly in the sea. The men were in chest-high water now, some of them carrying guns above their heads, walking through a sea that was already pink from the blood of other men in front of them.

Ishmael saw his friend Eric Bledsoe bleed to death. Fifty yards away he lay in the water begging in a soft voice for help. 'Help me, you guys, come on, you guys, help me, please.' Eric had grown up in Delaware; they'd got drunk together a lot in Wellington. Robert Newland wanted to run out to save him, but Lieutenant Bellows held him back; there was nothing to be done about it, Bellows pointed out, there was far too much gunfire for something like that, the only result would be two dead men, and everyone silently agreed. Ishmael pushed his body lower into the sand; he was not going to run to drag a wounded man to safety, though a part of him wanted to try.

The day continued like this, an unbroken series of pointless deaths, the American soldiers able neither to go forward nor back. In the early afternoon, Ishmael realized that the sweetish smell coming at him from the beach was the smell of dead soldiers. He was sick then and drank the last of his water. As far as he knew, no one else in his unit was even alive any more.

The situation did not improve as the day continued. Ishmael was ordered by an officer to regroup with other soldiers and was given a gun. In this process he did manage to find one of the men from his original group, Ernest Testaverde. However, by this time the Japanese had begun to attack again, trying to push them back into the sea. He was tired and thirsty, he could not really focus, and any excitement he might have felt at the beginning of the day had died inside of him. He wanted to live, he knew that now, but everything else was unclear.

At 1900 hours they tried to move up the beach with 300 other men. They were met by machine-gun fire from straight ahead in the trees. Ishmael never saw Ernest Testaverde get hit; later he found out, on making enquiries, that Ernest had been found with a hole in his head the size of a man's hand. Ishmael himself was hit high in the left arm, in the middle of the muscle. The bone cracked into a hundred tiny pieces that were driven up against his nerves and into the meat of his arm.

Ishmael was one of the lucky ones – although he could not think of himself as lucky. He was found by a medical team and taken back with a group of injured men to one of the ships seven miles out to sea from Betio. He travelled with a boy who had been shot below the stomach – the blood had covered his trousers. The boy could not speak; every few seconds he made a noise like an animal, breathing between his teeth. Ishmael asked him once if he was all right, but the boy died ten minutes before they were going to take him down to surgery.

Ishmael lost his arm on the ship. The man who cut it off had never done such a thing in his life before – normally his job was to give out medicine. Ishmael was not completely unconscious while this happened and he awoke to see his arm where it had been dropped in a corner. Ten years later he would still dream of that, the way his own fingers curled against the wall, how white and distant his arm looked, though nevertheless he recognized it there, a piece of rubbish on the floor. Somebody saw him staring at it and gave an order, and the arm was taken away. Ishmael found himself saying 'The Japs are... the Japs...' but he didn't quite know how to finish his words, he didn't quite know what he meant to say. 'I hate her, I hate that Jap, I hate her,' was all he could think of.

Chapter 15   Suspicion and Arrest

By two o'clock on the first afternoon of the trial, snow had covered all the island roads. Children on school buses and people going home or to work found themselves having to choose between digging their cars out of deep snow, or walking home and hoping that things would get better. Those who had lived on the island a long time knew that the storm was beyond their control. This storm might well be like others in the past that had caused them to suffer, or perhaps it might end beneath tonight's stars and give their children a mid-winter holiday.

Art Moran came back to the witness box after the midday break, and began to answer Alvin Hooks's questions once more.

'Sheriff Moran,' Hooks said at last. 'I have in my hand four pieces of rope of the sort fishermen use for tying up boats. Do you recognize them?'

Art Moran replied that he did and explained how he had taken the one marked 'A' from the left side of the defendant's boat, and that it was the same as all the other lines except for the one which was new. The new one, that was the one marked 'B'.

'And the other two exhibits?' asked Alvin Hooks. 'Where did you find them, Sheriff?'

The other ones came from Carl Heine's boat. One, marked 'C', was like all the other ones on that boat – from the right-hand side. The other one, 'D', was different. It was tied in a different way and was old, just like the ones on Kabuo Miyamoto's boat.

'So this line looks like the ones on the defendant's boat?' repeated Alvin Hooks.

'Exactly.'

'But you found it on the deceased's boat?'

'That's right.'

'And the defendant's boat – do I understand this right? – had a new line on the left-hand side, Sheriff, in the same position on the boat, but on the left-hand side?'

'That's right, Mr Hooks. There was a new section of rope there.'

'Sheriff,' Alvin Hooks said, 'if the defendant had tied up to Carl Heine's boat, would these two ropes in question be opposite each other?'

'Yes, they would. And if he, Miyamoto there, had left in a hurry, he could have left a rope behind tied in exactly that place.'

'And what led you to investigate the defendant in the first place? Why did you think to look around his boat and to notice something like this new rope?'

Art told him that his investigation into the death of Carl Heine had led him, quite naturally, to ask questions of Carl's relatives. He'd gone to see Etta Heine, and from her to Ole Jurgensen. After that, he felt he had to go and search Kabuo Miyamoto's boat.

In order to have the right to make such a search, Art Moran had gone to Judge Fielding. He had gone to see him at the end of the afternoon and had persuaded him that he had good reasons for seeing Miyamoto this way. Judge Fielding was not happy about him making the search – there was still nothing to say that Carl Heine's death was not an accident. And he insisted that the sheriff should only search the boat – not worry the wife and children yet.

'A limited search,' he said. 'The murder weapon, Art, and nothing else. I won't have you troubling this man's private life unnecessarily.'

When Kabuo Miyamoto came to the waterside that evening, carrying a battery for the *Islander*, he saw thirty or forty seagulls sitting on his boat. He started to get on, and they seemed to rise as one being, a great white mass of wings beating above his head. They flew overhead five or six times in a great circle that took in the entire port, then settled on the sea.

Kabuo's heart worked hard in his chest – he had never seen anything like this before and did not know whether it was a good or bad sign. He went down into the boat and opened the battery cover. He slid his new battery into place and connected it. Finally he started the engine.

Sheriff Moran and his deputy arrived as Kabuo was preparing to leave the port. The sheriff told him they had to search the boat. Kabuo had asked why and was told that they had come because of the death of Carl Heine, that they were looking for a murder weapon. Kabuo read the document that gave them authority and told them to go ahead – he'd not killed Carl Heine and they were wasting their time.

After half an hour Kabuo said, 'There's nothing to see. You guys are wasting your time and mine. I need to get out there fishing.'

It was then that Abel noticed the long-handled gaff that Kabuo – like other fishermen – kept to pull large fish into the boat.

'Look at this,' Abel said, holding up the heavy three-and-a-half foot gaff with the steel hook on one end. He gave it to Art Moran.

'There's blood on it,' he pointed out.

'Fish blood,' said Kabuo. 'I hook fish with that.'

'What's fish blood doing on the end of the handle?' Art asked. 'I'd expect maybe to see blood on the hook, but on this end? Where your hand goes? Fish blood?'

'Sure,' said Kabuo. 'It gets on your hands, Sheriff. Ask any of these fishermen about that.'

The sheriff took a cloth from the back pocket of his trousers and held the gaff in it. 'I'm going to take this and have it tested,' he said, and handed it to Abel Martinson. 'I wonder if I could get you to stay in tonight, stay off the water until you hear from me. I know you want to go out and fish, but I wonder if you shouldn't stay in tonight. Go home. Wait and see. Wait there until you hear from me. Because otherwise I'm going to have to arrest you now. Hold you in connection with all this.'

'I didn't kill him,' repeated Kabuo Miyamoto. 'And I can't afford not to fish. I can't let the boat sit doing nothing on a night like this and—'

'Then you're under arrest,' cut in Art Moran. 'Because there's no way I'm letting you go out there. In a half-hour you might be in Canada.'

Sherlock Holmes, he remembered Horace Whaley had said. All right, in the end he had played Sherlock Holmes, yes: it had been a sort of game. He had not really expected to find anything other than that Carl Heine had drowned. But maybe he did have a murder on his hands.

'You're under arrest,' repeated Art Moran, 'in connection with the death of Carl Heine.'

Chapter 16   Blood Tests and Murder Weapons

On the morning of December 7th, the second day of the trial, it was still snowing hard, but people had nevertheless made the effort to come to the courthouse and the windows were already covered with steam as their wet coats started to dry out.

As soon as Judge Fielding had sat down, he turned to Alvin Hooks.

'A new day,' he told him, 'but still your day in court, Mr Prosecutor. Go ahead. Call your witness.'

The next prosecution witness was Dr Sterling Whitman, the specialist in blood analysis at the Anacortes General Hospital.

'Now, Dr Whitman,' said Alvin Hooks, 'on the evening, the late evening, of September 16th of this year, the sheriff of this county brought you a tool used in fishing, did he not, and asked you to test the blood he found on it. Is that correct, Dr Whitman?'

'It is.'

'All right,' he said. 'Now, Dr Whitman. I'm returning to you your investigative report concerning this tool. Would you please summarize your findings for the court?'

'Certainly,' Sterling Whitman said, pulling uncomfortably at his sleeve. 'Number one was that the blood on the handle was human blood. Number two was that the blood was of a sort we can describe as B positive, Mr Hooks.'

'Anything else significant?' asked Alvin Hooks.

'Yes,' said Sterling Whitman. 'The sheriff asked me to check our hospital records for the blood type of a fisherman named Carl Heine, Junior. I did so. We had the records on file. Mr Heine's blood type was B positive.'

'But, Dr Whitman,' said Alvin Hooks, 'many people must have this type of B positive blood. Can you say with any certainty that it was Carl Heine's?'

'No,' said Dr Whitman. 'I can't say that. But let me add that B positive is a relatively rare blood type. Statistically rare. Ten per cent of white males, at best.'

'I see,' said Alvin Hooks. 'One out of ten.'

'That's right,' said Sterling Whitman.

Having made this point, Alvin Hooks asked Dr Whitman about Kabuo Miyamoto's blood group. Dr Whitman told the court that it was an O negative blood type. The blood on the handle of the gaff could not have been his. Neither could it have been fish blood or the blood of any other animal.

Nels Gudmundsson got up slowly and carefully to ask his questions. After commenting on the weather and the difficult journey Dr Whitman had had getting to the island, he asked:

'This blood, where exactly did you find it? On what part, Dr Whitman? The handle end? The hook?'

'The handle,' the doctor answered. 'This end,' he pointed, 'opposite the hook.'

'Right here?' said Nels, and put his hand on it. 'You found blood on this wooden handle?'

'Yes.'

'How did you get your sample?' said Nels, still holding the gaff.

'I cut a part of the wood away. It's the normal way with dried blood.'

'And when you examined this, what did you see? Blood and wood?'

'Yes.'

'Anything else?'

'No. Nothing else.'

'Doctor,' said Nels Gudmundsson, 'were there no bits of bone, or hair, or skin?'

Sterling Whitman shook his head firmly. 'None,' he said. 'It was just as I have said. As I wrote in my report. Blood and wood only.'

Nels Gudmundsson waited for a moment, and then went back over the argument, reminding the jury that a small, fresh cut had been noticed on Carl Heine's hand and that in the case of a head wound you would expect to find more than blood on the weapon that had caused the wound.

'Given the fact,' he said, 'that the blood is on the handle of this tool, where a person would normally place their hand, and given the fact that you found only blood there and no bone or skin or hair, Doctor, the normal evidence of a head wound, I would think, what seems to you to be likely? That the blood on the handle, if it came from Carl Heine at all, came from his head or his hand?'

'I have no idea,' said Sterling Whitman. 'I'm a blood specialist, not a detective.'

'I'm not asking you to be a detective,' Nels said. 'I just want to know which is more probable.'

'The hand, I suppose,' Sterling Whitman replied. 'The hand, I guess, would be more probable than the head.'

'Thank you,' answered Nels Gudmundsson.

◆

Alvin Hooks called Army First Sergeant Victor Maples to the witness box after that morning's break. The buttons on Sergeant Maples's green uniform caught the courtroom light and held it. Sergeant Maples was overweight by thirty-five pounds but still looked impressive. The extra weight was nicely distributed; Maples was a powerful man. He had short, thick arms, no neck, and a boyish face.

Sergeant Maples had in his time trained thousands of men in hand-to-hand fighting; he was a specialist in this area. He explained to the court that at one point in the war he had been responsible for the training of Japanese Americans who had decided to join the army, and that, yes, he remembered Kabuo from among the thousands who'd come his way because of an unusual occurrence.

On the day in question, he had been explaining to one hundred Japanese American soldiers that, until they reached the battlefield, a wooden stick would be used instead of an actual weapon during training sessions.

The sergeant began to demonstrate basic techniques, and then asked for a volunteer. It was at this point, he told the court, that he came face to face with the defendant. A young man stepped forward into the ring of trainees and presented himself to the sergeant, bowing slightly and calling out loudly, 'Sir!' Sergeant Maples had been surprised by this and told the soldier so.

'Nobody in this army bows to nobody. It isn't military. Not American military. It isn't done.'

Sergeant Maples gave Miyamoto a wooden stick. Maples felt that there was something aggressive in the boy's appearance, a strong sense of confidence. Maples had seen many such boys come his way and was never frightened of them. He was only on rare occasions impressed or prepared to view them as his equal.

'When you are fighting, your enemy won't stand and wait for you,' he said now, looking the boy in the eye. 'It's one thing to practise on a bag full of sand, another to fight with a trained human being. In this case,' he told the gathered young soldiers, 'our volunteer will try to put into practice the avoidance skills we worked on this afternoon.'

He explained to the court how surprised he was, how thoroughly surprised, to find he couldn't hit the defendant. Kabuo Miyamoto hardly moved, and yet he slipped away from every attack. The one hundred trainees looked on in silence and gave no indication that they approved of either man. Sergeant Maples fought on with his wooden stick until Kabuo Miyamoto knocked it from his hands.

'Excuse me,' said Miyamoto. He knelt, picked up the stick, and handed it to the sergeant. Once again, he bowed.

'There's no need to bow,' the sergeant repeated. 'I already told you about that.'

'I do it out of habit,' said Kabuo Miyamoto. 'I'm used to bowing when I'm fighting somebody.' Then, suddenly, he brought his wooden stick up. He looked Sergeant Maples in the eye and smiled.

Sergeant Maples saw then that he had no alternative and fought with the defendant that afternoon. The fight lasted all of three seconds. On his first attack the sergeant was swept off his feet, then felt his head pinned to the ground with the point of the stick, then the stick was withdrawn, the defendant bowed and picked him up. 'Excuse me, Sergeant,' he'd said afterwards. 'Your stick, Sergeant.' He'd handed it to him.

After that Sergeant Maples took every opportunity he could to study *kendo* with an expert. Sergeant Maples wasn't stupid – he told the court this about himself without obvious humour – and so he learned all he could from Miyamoto, including the importance of bowing.

Sergeant Maples became a master with time and after the war taught *kendo* techniques to the army at Fort Sheridan. From his point of view as an expert in the ancient Japanese art of stick fighting, Sergeant Maples could say with certainty that the defendant was capable of killing a man far larger than himself with a fishing tool. In fact, there were few men known to him who could ably defend themselves against such an attack by Kabuo Miyamoto. He was, in Sergeant Maples's experience, a man both technically skilled at stick fighting and willing to use violence on another man. He had made, the record showed, an excellent soldier. No, it would not surprise Sergeant Victor Maples to hear that Kabuo Miyamoto had killed a man with a fishing gaff. He was highly capable of such an act.

Chapter 17   The Wife of the Deceased

Alvin Hooks, the prosecutor, knew well the value of Susan Marie Heine's beauty and her status as the dead man's wife. After all the other witnesses he had called, he would now finish matters by presenting the wife of the murdered man. She would persuade the jury to bring in a guilty verdict, not precisely with what she had to say, but because of who she was.

And it was true that she had little to say directly. She told the court how on the afternoon of Thursday, September 9th, Kabuo Miyamoto had stood at her doorstep and asked to speak with her husband. How she had given him coffee and how he and Carl, with Carl looking enormous beside the Japanese man, had gone to walk around the farm and talk. She told how Carl had not wanted to talk about the conversation, only that Kabuo had asked him to sell the seven acres of strawberry farm they had just agreed to buy from Ole Jurgensen.

'He wants seven of Ole's acres. He wants me to let Ole sell them to him. Or sell them to him myself. You know, step out of his way.'

When she asked him how he had replied, Carl said he had told Kabuo he would think about it, and so Kabuo went away. And now Carl did not know what to do. He did not want to anger his mother, he did not want to sell land to a Jap, but he did not want to do something that would harm someone who had been a friend before the war.

Telling all of this to the court, she remembered how the wind came up and moved the tops of the trees by the house, and she felt the unusual autumn warmth in it. Carl had told her more than once, he'd repeated it just the other day, how since the war he couldn't talk to people. Even his old friends were included in this, so that now Carl was a lonely man who understood land and work, boat and sea, his own hands, better than his mouth and heart. She remembered how she had felt sympathy for him and rubbed his shoulder gently and waited patiently beside him.

As she finished speaking, standing in the silent courtroom with her neighbours looking at her, she thought of that afternoon and of how she and Carl had made love in the shower room before he left to go fishing. He said he hoped to be back by 4 a.m. Then he left for the Amity Harbor docks, and she never saw him again.

Nels Gudmundsson kept at a distance from the witness box when it was his turn to question Susan Marie Heine: he did not want to appear ridiculous or disgusting by placing himself close beside a such a sadly beautiful woman. He was self-conscious about his age, self-conscious about the decline in his own sexual drive, the way in which ageing was robbing him day by day of any pleasure that his body could give him, or which he had been able to give to others.

'Mrs Heine,' he said, 'the defendant here appeared on your doorstep on Thursday, 9th September? Is that what I heard you say?'

'Yes, Mr Gudmundsson. That's right.'

'He asked to speak to your husband?'

'He did.'

'They walked outside in order to talk? They didn't speak in the house?'

'Correct,' said Susan Marie. 'They spoke outside. They walked our property for thirty or forty minutes.'

'I see,' said Nels. 'And you didn't accompany them?'

'No,' said Susan Marie. 'I didn't.'

'Did you hear any part of their conversation?'

'No.'

'Thank you,' Nels said. 'Because that concerns me. The fact that you've given evidence about this conversation without having heard any part of it.'

He pulled at the skin of his throat and turned his good eye on Judge Fielding. The judge, his head resting on his hand, looked back. He knew what Nels was implying. Unlike a normal witness, Susan Marie was allowed to report conversations that she had had with her dead husband. She could say things that would not be accepted as evidence from another witness. Alvin Hooks had been able to take advantage of this fact during his examination, and had created an impression in the minds of the jury of the difficulty between Kabuo and Carl Heine's family. Susan Marie had not done this on purpose, it was just something that a clever prosecution lawyer could do. Now Nels had to change that impression, show that things had not been so bad between the two men.

'Well then,' Nels said. 'To summarize, Mrs Heine. Your husband

and the defendant walked and talked, and you stayed behind. Is that right?'

'Yes, it is.'

'And after thirty to forty minutes your husband returned. Is that also right, Mrs Heine?'

'Yes, it is.'

'He reported to you a concern about how his mother might react if he sold to the defendant? Did I hear you say that, Mrs Heine?'

'You did.'

'But he was thinking about such a sale anyway?'

'That's right.'

'And he had said as much to the defendant?'

'Yes.'

'So, in other words, Mr Miyamoto left your house on the ninth having heard from your husband there was at least a possibility your husband would sell the seven acres to him.'

'That's right.'

'Your husband and the defendant — do I have this right? — had grown up together as boys?'

'As far as I know, yes.'

'Did your husband ever mention him as a neighbour, someone he knew from his youth?'

'Yes.'

'Did he tell you how they'd gone fishing together as boys of ten or eleven? Or that they'd played on the same high-school sports teams? That they rode the same school bus for many years? Any of that, Mrs Heine?'

'I suppose so,' Susan Marie said.

Nels then turned and looked fully at Kabuo Miyamoto, who still sat upright in his place at the defendant's table with his hands folded neatly in front of him. It was at this moment that the courtroom lights failed for a moment, came back on for another second or two, and then went out altogether. A tree had fallen on Piersall Road and knocked the power wires down.

Chapter 18   Out in the Snow

'Well timed,' Nels Gudmundsson said when the lights went out in the Island County Courthouse. 'I have no further questions for Mrs Heine, Your Honour.'

'Very well,' Judge Fielding replied. 'One thing at a time now. Patience, patience. Let's proceed in a sensible way, lights or no lights. Mr Hooks?'

Alvin Hooks rose and told the court that the prosecution had no further questions. 'In fact,' he added, 'the timing of this power cut is even more appropriate than my colleague for the defence suspects. Mrs Heine is our last witness.'

The jurors, some of them, moved in their seats and smiled. 'Very well, then,' said Lew Fielding. 'If that is the case, I think we can stop our proceedings until tomorrow in the hope that we will have electricity once more. Shall we say 8.30 a.m.?'

After the judge and the lawyers had gone out of the court, Ishmael Chambers also left. Given the snow and the power cut, he had many things to do. First to see that his mother was all right, and then to make arrangements for printing his paper if the power was going to be down for some time. He thought he might also go to the coastguard station and see if they had any new weather reports. As he walked down the main street Ishmael had to keep his head lowered; when he raised it the snow blew into his eyes. He could see, nevertheless, that there were no lights anywhere in Amity Harbor; the power was out completely. Four cars had been left in the middle of Hill Street, and one of them had hit a parked van, pushing in the driver's door.

Ishmael went into his office to check the phone – which was

dead – and then took his camera from a drawer so that he could take pictures of the storm damage. However important the trial was, the storm would still be at the front of people's minds.

His first stop was at Tom Torgerson's gas station, where he was able to get help to put the snow chains on his old DeSoto touring car. He then went down Main Street to Fisk's, where he bought a can of fuel for his mother's heater, and to the restaurant next door, where he picked up a couple of sandwiches.

At 2.35 that afternoon, Ishmael Chambers got into the DeSoto and set off carefully. On First Hill he heard his chains, felt them biting, and made his way down in first gear, leaning forward in his seat, and so made his way out of the darkened town. Center Valley's strawberry fields lay under nine inches of snow and were like a landscape in a dream, with no hard edges. He passed Ole Jurgensen's house, white wood smoke pouring from the chimney and disappearing on the wind – Ole, apparently, was keeping warm. At Center Valley Road and South Beach Drive Ishmael saw, ahead of him on the bend, a car that had failed to climb the hill. Ishmael recognized it as Fujiko and Hisao Imada's; in fact, Hisao was working with a spade at its back right wheel, which had slipped off the edge of the road.

Ishmael knew that Hisao would not ask for help, in part because San Piedro people never did, in part because that was his character. Ishmael decided to park at the bottom of the slope and walk the fifty yards up South Beach Drive, keeping his car well out of the road while he persuaded Hisao Imada to accept a ride from him. Ishmael had seen something else, too. On the far side of the car, with her own spade in hand, Hatsue worked without looking up. She was digging through the snow to the black earth of the cedar woods and throwing it underneath the tyres.

The car had been damaged when it came off the road and wasn't going anywhere, Ishmael could see that, but it took Hisao some time to accept this truth. After ten minutes of polite assistance Ishmael wondered aloud if his DeSoto wasn't the answer, and Hisao gave in to the idea as if to an unavoidable evil. He opened his car door, put in his spade, and came out with a bag of shopping and a can of heater fuel. Hatsue, for her part, went on with her digging, saying nothing and keeping to the far side of the car, and throwing black earth beneath the tyres.

At last her father went round the car and spoke to her once in Japanese. She stopped her work and came into the road then, and Ishmael was able to take a good look at her. He had spoken to her only the morning before in the second floor hallway of the Island County Courthouse, where she'd sat on a bench with her back to the window and told him four times to go away.

'Hello, Hatsue,' said Ishmael. 'I can give you a lift home, if you want.'

'My father says he's accepted,' Hatsue replied. 'He says he's grateful for your help.'

She followed her father and Ishmael down the hill to the DeSoto, still carrying her spade. Only once, driving and listening to Hisao, did Ishmael risk looking at Hatsue Miyamoto in his car mirror. She was very carefully looking out of the window, very carefully not looking at him. It seemed that all the years of their not talking, their not looking at one another as her children had grown and he had remained alone, had led to this moment in the car.

Then she did speak from the back seat, still looking out of the window. 'Your newspaper,' she said. That was all.

'Yes?' answered Ishmael. 'I'm listening.'

'The trial, Kabuo's trial, is unfair,' said Hatsue. 'You should talk about that in your newspaper.'

'What's unfair?' asked Ishmael slowly. 'What exactly is unfair? I'll be happy to write about it if you'll tell me.'

She was still staring out of the window at the snow, with a line of black wet hair against her cheek. 'It's all unfair,' she told him bitterly. 'Kabuo didn't kill anyone. It isn't in his heart to kill anyone. They brought in that sergeant to say he's a killer. That was unfair. Did you hear the things that man was saying? How Kabuo had it in his heart to kill? How horrible he is, a killer? Put it in your paper, about what that man said, how all of it was unfair. How the whole trial is unfair.'

Although Ishmael was not able to promise to write about this, saying that he was not a legal expert and could not criticize what the sergeant had said, he still felt he had an emotional advantage. He had spoken with her and she had spoken back, wanting something from him. The anger he had felt coming from her was better than nothing, he decided. It was an emotion of some sort they shared. After they arrived at her father's house he sat in the DeSoto and watched Hatsue walk away through the falling snow, carrying her spade on her shoulder. The thought came to him that maybe her husband was going out of her life, like he himself had once had to leave it, and that changed things between them.

After this unexpected meeting, Ishmael continued with his journey to the coastguard lighthouse on the rocks at Point White – a solid tower rising a hundred feet above the sea. After forty minutes of difficult driving Ishmael Chambers, in the last light of day, found himself seated in the office of the lighthouse chief officer, a large man named Evan Powell, who agreed to help him put together his story of the storm by letting him read through the records that they kept at the lighthouse.

One of the other officers, a man called Levant, led Ishmael down to the records room on the second floor, which was filled from floor to ceiling with wooden boxes and filing cabinets. It smelled of old paper and had not been dusted recently. 'Everything's dated,' Levant pointed out. 'That's how we do things, by dates, mainly. Radio communications, weather reports, everything's in here by date, I guess. There's a date on everything.'

'Are you the radioman?' Ishmael asked.

'I am now,' Levant said. 'I have been for the last couple of months or so – last guys got transferred, I moved up.'

'Is there a lot of record keeping with your job?'

'Sure,' Levant explained to him. 'We write them up, file them, they end up here in the cabinet. And that's all they're good for, seems like. They just take up space, that's all. No one pays any attention.'

'Looks like I'm going to be a while,' said Ishmael, looking around the room. 'Why don't you go about your business? If I need something I can find you.'

He was alone then with the mist of his breath in the lamp light and the boxes of records. Ishmael tried to concentrate on his work, but the image of Hatsue in the back seat of his car, her eyes meeting his in the mirror, carried him away into his memories; how he had tried to make contact with her when he came back from the war, how she had refused to touch him, refused to give him any of the friendship he so badly needed and which he felt he still had some right to.

'You'll think this is crazy,' Ishmael had said, the one time they had talked. 'But all I want is to hold you. All I want is just to hold you once and smell your hair, Hatsue. I think after that I'll be better.'

'Look,' she said, 'you know I can't. I can never touch you, Ishmael. Everything has to be over between us. We both have to put it all behind us and go on, live our lives. There's no halfway, from my point of view.'

And the years had passed. Now her husband was on trial for the murder of a man at sea. Thinking on these matters, the idea suddenly came to Ishmael that the coastguard records might contain something important to Kabuo's case. He put aside his weather records and began to search the cabinets, and a strange excitement grew in him.

It took Ishmael all of fifteen minutes to find what it was he wanted. It was in a filing cabinet to the right of the door, near the front of the third drawer down, records for 15th and 16th September of 1954. No wind, thick fog, calm. One ship through at 0120 hours, the S.S. *West Corona*, Greek owned, Liberian flag; she'd called in her position from out to the west, headed south towards Seattle. The radio messages were all written there: the *Corona* had put in a first call looking for the lighthouse radio signal. At 0126 hours that morning, in heavy fog, she had radioed the lighthouse for assistance. The *Corona* was out of the normal shipping lane, the radioman on duty at the lighthouse had reported back, and would have to go to the north-east, crossing Ship Channel Bank.

Ship Channel Bank. Where Dale Middleton, Vance Cope, and Leonard George had all seen Carl Heine with his net out the night he went into the sea. On that night an enormous ship had gone right through the fishing grounds, throwing before it a wall of water large enough to knock even a big man out of his small boat. Everything was there in three copies. They were signed by the radioman's assistant, a Seaman Philip Milholland – he'd written down the radio messages. Ishmael slipped three centre pages of Seaman Milholland's notes free and folded them so that the pages fitted neatly into his coat pocket, and he let them sit there, feeling them, calming himself down. Then he went up to the office.

'I'm done,' he said. 'There's just one more thing. Is Philip Milholland around somewhere? I want to talk to him.'

Levant shook his head. 'You know Milholland?' he said.

'Sort of,' said Ishmael.

'Milholland's gone. He got moved to Cape Flattery – Milholland and Robert Miller. Me and Smoltz, we started in together when they left back in September,' said Levant.

'So Milholland's gone,' said Ishmael.

'He left on 16th September.'

Nobody knows, thought Ishmael. The men who'd heard the *Corona*'s radio messages had gone somewhere else the next day. The record had gone into a folder, and the folder had gone into a filing cabinet in a room full of coastguard records. And who would find them there? They were as good as lost for ever, it seemed to Ishmael, and no one knew the truth of the matter: that on the night Carl Heine had drowned, stopping his watch at one forty-seven, a large ship went through Ship Channel Bank at one forty-two, just five minutes earlier, pushing before it a wall of water big enough to throw a large man, a man now thought to have been murdered, out of his small boat. And only one person knew this truth. That was the heart of it.

Chapter 19   Ishmael's Mother

Ishmael's mother lived on her own in a house about five miles from town. As he walked towards the back door, down the path his mother had dug through the snow, Ishmael felt the place in his coat pocket where Philip Milholland's coastguard notes lay folded against his leg. His mother came out of the warm, brightly-lit kitchen to help him bring the shopping in from the car. With the temperature down to minus twelve degrees they did not want things to freeze.

At fifty-six, Helen Chambers was the sort of country widow who makes a good life out of living alone. She had her reading circle and regular meetings with other women like herself, and she seemed quite satisfied with her own company. Ishmael found it hard to understand how she had been able to make something so positive with what seemed to be such unsatisfactory material. For her part, she still found it difficult that Ishmael was so turned against the world, that he had lost the sense of God that he had had as a child.

The wind blew against the window behind him and the snow outside fell fast. His mother had made soup and asked was he hungry now or did he want to wait? She was happy either way. They both looked out at the falling snow.

'Stay,' said his mother. 'Spend the night. Your room will be cold, but your bed should be fine. Don't go back out into all of that snow. Stay and be comfortable.'

He agreed to stay and she put the soup on. In the morning he would see about printing his newspaper; for now he was warm where he was. Ishmael sat with his hand in his coat pocket and wondered if he shouldn't just tell his mother about the coastguard notes he had stolen from the lighthouse and then drive carefully back into town to hand the notes over to Judge Fielding. But he did nothing. He sat watching the sky darken beyond the kitchen windows.

As his mother prepared their meal, he told her about the trial, describing what the different witnesses had said. In spite of the coastguard's notes, he could not stop himself from saying that he thought Kabuo was guilty. He told her how he had looked so proud, sitting there in court, still a Japanese soldier trained to kill and to take pride in killing. His mother reminded him that Kabuo had been in the US army, not the Japanese army, that he had fought and suffered like he himself had. But Ishmael could not accept this and felt a great emptiness that he could not explain to her. How was it that she had been able to find some way of living after her husband had died, when he could not learn to live with his own disaster?

'I'm unhappy,' he said. 'Tell me what to do.'

His mother made no reply at first. Instead she came to the table with his bowl of soup and set it down in front of him. She brought her own bowl to the table, too, and then a loaf of bread on a cutting board and a dish of butter and two spoons.

'You're unhappy,' she said, seating herself. She put her elbows down on the table and rested her chin against her hands. 'That you are unhappy, I have to say, is the most obvious thing in the world.'

'Tell me what to do,' repeated Ishmael.

'Tell you what to do?' his mother said. 'I can't tell you what to do, Ishmael. I've tried to understand what it's been like for you, having gone to war, having lost your arm, not having married or had children. I've tried to make sense of it all, believe me, I have, how it must feel to be you. But I have to say that, no matter how I try, I can't really understand you. There are other boys, after all, who went to war and came back home and pushed on with their lives. They found girls and married and had children and raised families despite whatever was behind them. But you, you went cold, Ishmael. And you've stayed that way all these years. And I haven't known what to do or say about it or how I might help you in some way. I've wanted you to be happy, Ishmael. But I haven't known what to do.'

They ate their soup and bread in silence. The candle on the table threw a circle of light across their food, and outside, through the window, the snow on the ground caught the moonlight beyond the clouds and held it so that it covered everything. Ishmael tried to enjoy the small pleasures of warmth and light and bread. He did not want to tell his mother about Hatsue Miyamoto and how he had, many years ago, felt certain they would be married. He did not want to tell her about the hollow cedar tree where they'd met so many times. He had never told anybody about those days; he had worked hard to forget them. Now the trial had brought all of that back.

As they ate, they talked about his father and how he had got over his experience of fighting in the First World War, how he had been able to make a life. Ishmael told his mother about how he had tried, how he had worked to keep the paper going, to remake his own life. But he could not bring himself to talk about the things that really mattered, and so she could not help him.

Walking through the house as he prepared to go to bed, Ishmael remembered all the years of living here, nights of listening to the radio with his father, reading late at night with a light under his bed covers. He remembered his father, half-asleep at the end of the evening with a book open in his hands. In the cupboard in his bedroom were boxes full of his childhood – his books, his essays from high school, his collection of beach stones; they were the things of another time. And between the pages of a book on boats he'd been given on his thirteenth birthday, the letter from Hatsue with the upside-down stamp. He sat on the edge of his bed and read·

Dear Ishmael,

These things are very difficult to say – I can't think of anything more painful to me than writing this letter to you. I am now more than 500 miles away, and everything appears to me different from what it was when I was with you last on San Piedro. I have been trying to think clearly about everything, and here is what I've discovered.

I don't love you, Ishmael. I can think of no more honest way to say it. From the very beginning, when we were little children, it seemed to me something was wrong. Whenever we were together I knew it. I felt it inside of me. I loved you and I didn't love you at the very same moment, and I felt troubled and confused. Now everything is obvious to me and I feel I'm telling you the truth. When we met that last time in the cedar tree and I felt your body against mine, I knew with certainty that everything was wrong. I knew we could never be right together and that soon I would have to tell you so. And now, with this letter, I am telling you. This is the last time I will write to you. I am not yours any more.

I wish you the very best, Ishmael. Your heart is large and you are gentle and kind, and I know you will do great things in this world. But now I must say goodbye to you. I am going to move on with my life as best I can, and I hope that you will, too.

Sincerely,

HATSUE IMADA.

He read it over a second time, and then a third. Ishmael shut his eyes and thought back to that moment in the cedar tree when he had wanted her, really wanted her, and how he had not been able to predict how good that would feel. And the funny thing was that this was the last thing in the world that she wanted. How was it that two such different truths could come out of the same gentle moment?

Thinking about this, he decided he would write the article Hatsue wanted him to write in the pages of the *Review*. It was perhaps not the way in which his father would proceed, but so be it: he was not his father. His father, of course, would have gone hours earlier directly to Lew Fielding in order to show him the coastguard shipping lane records for the night of September 15th. But not Ishmael, not now, no. Those records would stay in his pocket. Tomorrow, he would write the article she wanted him to write, in order to put her in his debt, and then, after the trial was finished, he would speak with her as one who had taken her side and she would have no choice but to listen. That was the way, that was the method. Sitting by himself in the cold of his old bedroom, her letter in his hand, he began to imagine it.

Chapter 20   Hatsue Miyamoto's Story

At eight in the morning on the third day of the trial, a dozen tall candles now lighting the courtroom as in a church, Nels Gudmundsson called his first witness. The wife of the accused man, Hatsue Miyamoto, came forward from the last row of seats with her hair tightly bound to the back of her head and held up under a simple hat that threw a shadow over her eyes.

Nels's first questions concerned events on the day Kabuo talked to Carl Heine about the land he had bought from Ole Jurgensen.

'It's Thursday, 9th September,' Nels Gudmundsson said to her. 'It's two days since your husband spoke with Ole Jurgensen about the sale of the farm; two long days have passed since he learned that Carl Heine had bought his father's farm. Can you tell the court what happened on that day, Mrs Miyamoto?'

'What happened?'

'He went to talk to Carl Heine – am I correct? – as Susan Marie Heine told us yesterday. She said that the two of them discussed the seven acres and the possibility that your husband might purchase them. She has also told us that Carl did not give your husband a definite answer. It was her understanding that Carl had encouraged your husband to believe that a possibility of an agreement existed. Now, does that seem accurate to you, Mrs Miyamoto? On the afternoon of 9th September, after his talk with Carl Heine, did your husband still seem hopeful?'

'More hopeful than ever,' said Hatsue. 'He came home from his conversation with Carl Heine more hopeful and more eager than ever. He told me that he felt closer to getting the family land back than he had in a long, long time. I felt hopeful, too, at that point. I was hopeful it would all work out.'

And she *had* been hopeful. She could remember the worst times. How one night just after Kabuo had come back home at the end of the war he had gone out the rain and come back wet and cold carrying a dirty cloth bag. He had knelt on the floor and opened the bag and taken a strawberry plant from it while the rain hammered against the roof and beat against the side of their house. Kabuo took out a second strawberry plant and brought them both into the light over the table where she could look at them closely if she wanted to. He held them out to her, and she looked at the plants in his hands – and also saw the muscles just beneath his skin and how strong his wrists and fingers were.

'My father planted the fathers of these plants,' Kabuo said to her angrily. 'We lived as children by the fruit they produced. Do you understand what I am saying?'

'Come to bed,' answered Hatsue. 'Take a bath, dry yourself, and come back to bed,' she said.

She got up and left the kitchen table. She knew that he could see the shape their new baby was making. 'You're going to be a father soon,' she reminded him, pausing in the doorway. 'I hope that will make you happy, Kabuo. I hope it will help you to bury all of this. I don't know how else I can help you.'

'I'll get the farm back,' Kabuo had answered over the noise of the rain. 'We'll live there. We'll grow strawberries. It will be all right. I'm going to get my farm back.'

That had been many years ago – nine years, or nearly. They'd saved as much money as they could, until they had enough to buy their own house. Hatsue wanted to move from the broken-down cottage they rented at the end of Bender's Spring Road, but Kabuo had made her agree that the better move was to buy a gill-netting boat. Within a year or two, he said, they would double their money, own the boat altogether, and have enough left over for a land payment. Ole Jurgensen was getting old, he said. He would want to sell before long.

And Kabuo had fished as well as he could, but he was not really born to fish. There was money in fishing and he wanted the money; he was strong, determined and a hard worker, but the sea, in the end, made no sense to him. They had not doubled their money or even come close, and they did not own the *Islander* yet. Kabuo only pressed himself harder and measured his life according to his success at bringing salmon home. On every night that he did not catch fish he felt his dream become more distant, and the strawberry farm he wanted moved further out of his reach. He blamed himself and grew short-tempered with his wife, and this deepened the wounds in their marriage. Hatsue felt she did him no favours by accepting his self-pity, and he hated her sometimes for this. It was difficult for her to tell these moments from the deeper pain of his war wounds. Besides, she had three children now, and it was necessary to turn her attention towards them and to give to them a part of what she had once given to her husband. The children, she hoped, would soften him. She hoped that through them he might become less set on the dream of a different life. She knew that had happened in her own heart.

Yes, it would be good to live in a nicer house and to walk out into the sweet smell of berries on a June morning, to stand in the wind and smell them. But this house and this life were what she had, and there was no point in always reaching for something other. Gently she tried to tell him so, but Kabuo insisted that just around the corner lay a different life and a better one, that it was simply a matter of catching more salmon, of waiting for Ole Jurgensen to slow down, of saving their money.

◆

Nels pushed himself upright again and began, slowly, to walk up and down before the jurors, thinking in silence for a moment. In the quiet the wind pushed against the windows. With no overhead lights the courtroom seemed greyer and duller than ever. The smell of snow was in the air.

'Why did you feel hopeful, Mrs Miyamoto, if I might ask? Especially after all of the problems between Etta Heine and Kabuo's family.'

'My husband felt that it was Carl's decision, not his mother's, this time. And Carl had been his friend long ago. Carl would do what was right.'

'Mrs Miyamoto,' Nels continued, 'your husband had his

conversation with Carl Heine on the afternoon of Thursday, 9th September. On the following Thursday, 16th September, Carl Heine was found drowned in his fishing net out in White Sand Bay. A week passed between these two events. My question is whether your husband said or did anything about the seven acres in question during the week between the ninth and the sixteenth?'

Well, explained Hatsue, Kabuo felt there was nothing to do, that the next move was Carl's, that it was Carl who had to come forward. It was Carl who had to think about things and come to some conclusion. It was Carl's heart that was now in question. Did Carl feel responsible for the actions of his family? Did he understand his obligations? It was dishonourable, anyway, Kabuo had added, to approach Carl once again with the same tired question; he did not wish to beg. It was best to be patient in such a matter.

On the morning of the sixteenth, Hatsue told the court, while she was boiling water for tea, he pushed through the door in his rubber boots and explained how he had seen Carl out at sea, helped Carl with a dead battery in the fog, and the two of them had shaken hands on the matter. They'd come to an agreement about the seven acres. Eighty-four hundred dollars, eight hundred down. The Miyamotos' land was Kabuo's again, after all these years.

But later that day, at one o'clock in the afternoon, an assistant at Petersen's general store – it was Jessica Porter – told Hatsue about the terrible accident that had taken Carl Heine's life while he fished that evening. He'd been found in his net, out in White Sand Bay.

Alvin Hooks began his cross-examination sitting on the edge of the prosecutor's table and crossing his well-polished shoes in front of him as though he were relaxing on a street corner. His hands held together, he turned his head to the right for a moment and studied Hatsue Miyamoto. 'You know,' he said, 'it's been interesting hearing from you. On this matter of the morning of the sixteenth in particular. This story you've just told us about boiling water when the defendant came through your kitchen door, terribly excited, and told you about his conversation at sea, how he and Carl Heine came to some sort of agreement? I found this all quite interesting.'

He stopped and studied her for another moment. Then he began to nod. He put his hand to his head and turned his eyes toward the ceiling.

'Mrs Miyamoto,' he sighed, 'was I fair just now in describing your husband's state of mind as "terribly excited" on the morning of the sixteenth, the morning Carl Heine was murdered? Did he come home on that morning "terribly excited"?'

'I would use that phrase, yes,' said Hatsue. 'He was terribly excited, certainly.'

'He didn't seem himself? His state of mind was – upset? He seemed to you somehow... different?'

'Excited,' answered Hatsue. 'Not upset. He was excited about getting his family's land back.'

'All right, so he was "excited",' Alvin Hooks said. 'And he told you this story about stopping at sea to help Carl Heine with a... dead battery or something. Is that correct, Mrs Miyamoto?'

'That's correct.'

'He said that he tied up to Carl Heine's boat to lend Carl a battery?'

'That's right.'

'And that during this friendly act he and Carl discussed the seven acres they'd been arguing about until that point? Is that right? And that somehow Carl agreed to sell it to him? For eighty-four hundred dollars or something? Is that all correct? Do I have it right?'

'You do,' said Hatsue. 'That's what happened.'

'Mrs Miyamoto,' said Alvin Hooks. 'Did you, by any chance, repeat this story to anyone? Did you, for example, call a friend or a relative to deliver the happy news? Did you let your friends and family know that your husband had come to terms with Carl Heine in the middle of the night on his fishing boat, that you would soon be moving to seven acres of strawberry land, starting a new life, anything like that?'

'No,' said Hatsue. 'I didn't.'

'Why not?' asked Alvin Hooks. 'Why didn't you tell anyone? It seems like the sort of thing that would be news. It would seem you might tell your mother, for example, or your sisters perhaps – someone.'

Hatsue moved unhappily in her chair and brushed at her blouse front. 'Well,' she said, 'we heard about how Carl Heine had . . . just recently died a few hours after Kabuo came home. Carl's accident – that changed how we thought. It meant there was nothing to tell anyone. The situation was no longer straightforward.'

'The situation was no longer straightforward,' said Alvin Hooks, settling his arms across his chest. 'When you heard that Carl Heine had died, you decided not to talk about the matter? Is that what you're saying, am I correct?'

'You're misinterpreting,' complained Hatsue. 'We just–'

'I'm not interpreting or misinterpreting,' Alvin Hooks cut in. 'I only want to know what the facts are, we all want to know what the facts are, Mrs Miyamoto, that's what we're doing here. So please, madam, if I might ask again, did you decide not to talk about your husband's night at sea, his meeting with Carl Heine? Did you decide not to talk about this matter?'

'There was nothing to talk about,' said Hatsue. 'What news could I announce to my family? The situation was no longer straightforward.'

'Worse than that,' said Alvin Hooks. 'On top of your husband's business deal going sour, a man, we might note, had died. A man had died, let us understand, with the side of his skull beaten in. Did it occur to you, Mrs Miyamoto, to come forward with the information you had about this and inform the sheriff? Did you ever think it might be proper to share what you knew, your husband's night at sea, this battery business, and so on, with the sheriff of Island County?'

'We thought about it, yes,' said Hatsue. 'We talked about it all afternoon that day, if we should go to the sheriff and tell him, if we should talk about things. But in the end we decided not to, you see – it looked very bad, it looked like murder, Kabuo and I understood that. We understood that he could end up here, on trial, and that's exactly what has happened. That's exactly how it has turned out, you see. You've charged my husband with murder.'

'Well, of course,' said Alvin Hooks. 'I can see how you felt. I can see how you might be very concerned that your husband would be charged with murder. But if, as you imply, the truth was on your side, what in the world were you worried about? Why, if the truth was really with you, why on earth, Mrs Miyamoto, why not go immediately to the sheriff and tell him everything you know?'

'We were afraid,' said Hatsue. 'Silence seemed better. To come forward seemed like a mistake.'

'Well,' said Alvin Hooks, 'the mistake, it seems to me, was in not coming forward. The act of a decent citizen, it seems to me, is to help a community discover what has happened if one of its sons dies. But you and your husband thought that silence seemed better. I am afraid, Mrs Miyamoto, that your silence on 16th September is clearer evidence to this court than any words you might wish to use now. Your Honour, I have no further questions of this witness.'

In the silence that followed this attack Hatsue made an effort to prevent tears from coming to her eyes. She had no further right to speak in defence of her husband and must return to her seat. She stood up without saying another word and went to her seat at the back of the courthouse where, adjusting her hat, she sat down. A few citizens in the gallery, including Ishmael Chambers, could not help turning to look at her, but she made no move to acknowledge them. She stared straight ahead and said nothing.

Chapter 21   Kabuo Miyamoto's Story

The storm winds blew against the courtroom windows and shook them in their frames so violently it seemed the glass would break. For three days and nights the citizens in the gallery had listened to the wind beat against their houses and struggled against it to make their way to and from the courthouse. They had not yet become used to it. It seemed unlikely that a wind should blow so consistently for days on end. It made them angry and impatient. The snow was one thing, falling as it did, but the noise of the storm, the force of it against their faces – everyone wished unconsciously that it would come to an end and give them peace. They were tired of listening to it.

Kabuo Miyamoto, the accused man, had not heard the wind at all from his cell. Instead, all that third night Kabuo had considered the mess he had got himself into. He thought about why he had refused to tell Nels everything that had happened when they had talked together before the trial. Maybe it was like Nels had said after their second or third meeting – because his parents were Japanese, nobody would believe him anyway. It was more or less the truth. Kabuo and Hatsue had not wanted to speak because they thought no one would accept their word.

On the night Carl Heine died, Kabuo had gone fishing with an added sense of purpose. Every salmon he caught from now on would help him pay for his farm. As the sky darkened he ate three rice balls, some fish and two apples from a wild tree behind their house. It was already starting to get foggy. By 8.30 he had begun fishing. From the lighthouse station far to the east he could hear the low, steady sound of the fog signal. Kabuo laid his net out north to south, hoping all the time that he was not moving into the shipping lane that ran near to the island at this point. In such fog, there was always the danger of a larger ship coming down on a fishing boat. Still, he thought to himself, he'd done all he could. He'd set his net as well as possible. There was nothing to do now but be patient. As his boat moved slowly, drawing the net tight behind, he listened to the radio, hearing complaints from other fishermen about the fog, the lack of fish, the danger from larger boats. Kabuo left his radio on; he wanted to hear about it if a large boat came down this side of the island and put in a call to the lighthouse.

At 10.30 he started to pull in his net. He was happy to find he was bringing good salmon in, big ones – mostly over ten and eleven pounds. There were fifty-eight salmon, he counted, for this first run, and he felt grateful about them. He looked down at them with satisfaction and calculated their value. He thought of the journey they'd made to him and how their lives, perhaps, would buy his farm back. By now it was close to 11.30, if his watch was right, and he decided to motor west again to start his second run. As the *Islander* moved through the fog, he used his horn to signal his position. After about half an hour of this slow progress he heard another air-horn over to the right. Whoever it was, he was close.

Kabuo stopped his engine, his heart beating hard in his chest. The other man was too near, seventy-five yards, a hundred at best, out there in the fog, his motor cut. Kabuo sounded his horn again. In the silence that followed came a reply, this time a man's voice, clear and calm, a voice he recognized. 'I'm over here,' it called across the water. 'I'm dead in the water, I've got no power.'

And this was how he had found Carl Heine, his batteries dead, in need of another man's assistance. There Carl stood in the *Islander*'s lights, a big man with an oil lamp in one hand and an air-horn held in the other. 'I'm dead in the water,' he'd said again, when Kabuo threw him a rope. 'My batteries are no good. Both of them.'

'All right,' said Kabuo. 'Let's tie up. Mine are good – and the spare.'

'Thank God for that,' answered Carl. 'It's lucky you found me.'

'Hope we're not in the shipping lane,' said Kabuo, looking up at the *Susan Marie*'s mast. 'Looks like you put a lamp up.'

'Tied it up there just a bit ago,' said Carl. 'Best I could do, seems like. Lost my radio when the batteries went, couldn't call anyone. Couldn't do anything to help myself. Lamp's probably useless in this fog, but anyway I've got it up there. It's all the lights I've got just now, that and the one I've been carrying. Probably isn't worth nothing to nobody.'

'I've got two batteries,' Kabuo answered. 'We'll use one and get you started.'

'Appreciate that,' said Carl. 'Thing is I run size 8s see. I suppose you run off size 6s.'

'I do,' said Kabuo. 'But it'll work if you've got room.'

'I'll measure,' said Carl. 'Then we'll know.'

He crossed back over to his boat, and Kabuo hoped that there was part of Carl wanting to discuss the land that lay between them silently. Carl would have to say something one way or the other simply because the two of them were at sea together, tied boat to boat but to nothing else, sharing the same problem.

Once Carl had checked that the new battery would fit if they bent part of the metal holder, Kabuo came onto his boat carrying his gaff. 'I'll bring this,' he said. 'We can hammer with it.'

They worked together to get the battery in place. Carl cut his hand on the metal holder but did not stop to suck the wound until he had finished hammering. Once they had checked that everything worked, Kabuo told him he could return the battery at the harbour. They might as well get back to trying to catch fish. As he stood there, holding his gaff in his hand once more, Carl told him to stop, said there were things they needed to talk about.

'Seven acres,' said Carl Heine. 'I'm wondering what you'd pay for 'em, Kabuo. Just wondering, that's all.'

'What are you selling them for?' Kabuo asked. 'Why don't we start with what you want for them? I guess I'd rather start there.'

'Did I say I was selling?' Carl asked. 'Didn't say one way or the other, did I? But if I was, I guess I'd have to figure they're mine and you want 'em pretty bad. Guess I ought to charge you a small fortune, but then maybe you'd want your battery back, leave me out here in the fog.'

'The battery's in,' Kabuo answered, smiling. 'That's separate from the rest of things. Besides, you'd do the same for me.'

'I *might* do the same for you,' said Carl. 'I have to warn you about that, chief. I'm not screwed together like I used to be. It isn't like it was before.'

'All right,' said Kabuo. 'If you say so.'

'Hell,' said Carl, 'I'm not saying what I mean. Look, I'm sorry, OK? I'm sorry over this whole business. If I'd been around, it wouldn't have happened how it did. My mother pulled it off, I was out at sea, fighting you Japs–'

'I'm an American,' Kabuo cut in. 'Just like you or anybody. Am I calling you a Nazi,* you big Nazi bastard? I killed men who looked just like you, pig-fed Germans. I've got their blood on my soul, Carl, and it doesn't wash off very easily. So don't you talk to

* Nazi: a member of the National Socialist Party led by Adolf Hitler; it was used as a name for German soldiers during the Second World War.

87

me about Japs, you big Nazi bastard.'

He still held the gaff tightly in one hand, and he became aware of it now. Carl looked at him. 'I am a bastard,' he said finally, and stared out into the fog. 'I'm a big Nazi bastard, and you know what else, Kabuo? I've still got your fishing pole. I kept it all these years. I hid it after my mother tried to make me return it to your house. You went off to prison camp, I caught a lot of fish with it. It's still in my room at home.'

'Leave it there,' said Kabuo Miyamoto. 'I forgot all about that fishing pole. You can have it. To hell with it.'

'To hell with that,' said Carl. 'It's been driving me crazy all these years. I open up my cupboard and there it is, your fishing pole.'

'Give it back, if you want,' said Kabuo. 'But I'm telling you you can keep it, Carl. That's why I gave it to you.'

'All right,' said Carl. 'Then that settles it. Twelve hundred an acre and that's final. That's what I'm paying Ole, see. That's the going price for strawberry land, go and have a look around.'

'That's eighty-four hundred for the lot,' answered Kabuo. 'How much are you going to want now?'

Carl Heine turned and put out his hand. Kabuo put the gaff down and took it. They did not shake so much as hold on like fishermen who know they can go no further with words and must communicate in another fashion. So they stood there at sea in the fog, and locked their hands together, and there was the blood from Carl's cut on their hands. They did not mean for it to say too much, and at the same time they wished for it to say everything. They moved away from this more quickly than they desired but before the embarrassment was too much for them. 'A thousand down,' said Carl Heine. 'We can sign papers tomorrow.'

'Eight hundred,' said Kabuo, 'and it's a deal.'

◆

When Kabuo had finished telling his story on the witness stand, Alvin Hooks rose and stood before him.

'Mr Miyamoto,' he began, 'for the life of me I can't understand why you didn't tell this story from the start. After all, don't you think it might have been your duty to come forward with all of this information?'

The accused man looked at the jurors, ignoring Alvin Hooks entirely, and answered quietly and evenly in their direction, as if there were no one else present. 'You must understand,' he said to them, 'that I heard nothing about the death of Carl Heine until one o'clock on the afternoon of 16th September and that within just a few hours of my having heard of it Sheriff Moran arrested me. There was no time for me to voluntarily come forward with the events as I have just explained them. I–'

Alvin Hooks came and stood between Kabuo and the jury and started to go back over the events from 16th September. He told Kabuo how his problem was that he had changed his story. First he had told the sheriff he knew nothing about Carl, had not seen him that night. Then he told this story about meeting the man at sea and making an agreement with him over the land.

Alvin Hooks held his chin in his fingers. 'You're a hard man to trust, Mr Miyamoto,' he sighed. 'You sit before us with no expression, keeping a face like a Japanese officer through–'

'Objection!' cut in Nels Gudmundsson, but Judge Lew Fielding was already sitting upright and looking severely at Alvin. 'You know better than that, Mr Hooks,' he said. 'Either ask questions that count for something or have a seat and be done with it. Shame on you,' he added.

Alvin Hooks crossed the courtroom one more time and sat down at the prosecutor's table. He picked up his pen and, turning it in his fingers, looked out of the window at the falling snow, which seemed to be slowing finally. 'I can't think of anything more,' he said. 'The witness is free to go now.'

Kabuo Miyamoto rose in the witness box and looked out at the snow, standing so that the citizens in the courtroom saw him fully, a proud Japanese man standing before them. They noted how he stood straight, and the strength in his chest. The citizens in the court were reminded of photographs they had seen of Japanese soldiers. Although the man before them was honest in appearance, the shadows played across his face in a way that made their angles harden, and there was no sense of softness in him anywhere, no part of him that could be touched. He was, they decided, not like them at all, and the calm manner in which he watched the snow fall made this suddenly clear to them.

Chapter 22   The End of the Trial

Alvin Hooks, in his final words to the court, described the accused man as a cold-blooded murderer, one who had decided to kill another man and had carried out his plan faithfully. He had, quite simply, decided to end the life of another man who stood between him and the land he wanted. If Carl Heine was dead, Ole would sell him the seven acres. And so it was that he followed Carl to the fishing grounds at Ship Channel Bank. He followed him out, set his net above him, and watched while the fog hid everything. It was then, in the middle of the night, that he called for the help which he knew Carl Heine would give. Carl, he must have said, I am sorry for what has come between us, but here on the water, alone in the fog, I am asking you for your help. Please don't leave me like this.

'Imagine,' Alvin Hooks begged the jurors, leaning towards them with his hands outstretched like a man praying to God. 'Imagine this good man stopping to help his enemy in the middle of the night at sea. He ties his boat to his enemy's boat, and his enemy jumps aboard with a fishing gaff and strikes a blow to his head. And so this good man falls dead, or nearly dead, that is. He is unconscious and badly wounded.

'Let us imagine, too,' continued Alvin Hooks, 'the defendant rolling Carl Heine over the side and the sound of the body hitting the black night water. The sea closes over Carl Heine, stopping his pocket watch at 1.47, recording the time of his death, and the defendant stands watching the place where the waters have closed, leaving no sign behind. But there is one thing that the defendant has not thought of. Carl's clothing becomes caught in his own net and he hangs there, under the sea, the evidence of Kabuo Miyamoto's crime waiting to be discovered. It is one of three things the defendant hasn't counted on – the body itself, the bloody fishing gaff, and the rope he'd left behind at this scene of murder.

'Now he sits in this court before you,' Alvin Hooks told the jurors. 'Here he is in a court of law with the evidence and the facts before him. There is no uncertainty any more and you must do your duty to the people of Island County.

'This is not a happy occasion,' Alvin Hooks reminded them. 'We are talking about murder in the first degree. We're talking about justice. We're talking about looking clearly at the defendant and seeing the truth in him and in the facts present in this case. Take a good look, ladies and gentlemen, at the defendant sitting over there. Look into his eyes, consider his face, and ask yourselves what your duty is as citizens of this community.'

Just as he had throughout the trial, Nels Gudmundsson rose with his old man's awkwardness that was painful for the citizens to observe. By now they had learned to be patient with him as he cleared his throat and coughed. The jurors had noted how his left eye floated and how the light played against its dull, glassy surface. They watched him now as he gathered himself up and cleared his throat to speak.

In measured tones, as calmly as he could, Nels went over the facts as he understood them: Kabuo Miyamoto had gone to Ole Jurgensen to inquire about his land. Mr Jurgensen had directed him to Carl Heine, and Kabuo had looked for Carl. They had spoken and Kabuo had come to believe that Carl was thinking about the matter. And so, believing this, he waited. He waited and, on the evening of 15th September, chance brought him through the fog at Ship Channel Bank to where Carl was in difficulty at sea. Kabuo had done what he could in these circumstances to assist the friend he had known since childhood, a boy he'd fished with years earlier. And finally, said Nels, they spoke of the land and resolved this matter between them. Then Kabuo Miyamoto went on his way again and fished until the morning. And the next day he found himself arrested.

There was no evidence presented, Nels Gudmundsson told the jurors, to suggest that the accused man had planned a murder or that he'd gone to sea in search of blood. The state had not produced a single piece of evidence to suggest the act had been planned. The state had not proved beyond a reasonable doubt that the crime the defendant had been charged with had in fact occurred. There was more than reasonable doubt, added Nels, but reasonable doubt was all that was needed. There was reasonable doubt, he emphasized, so the jury could not find him guilty.

'The counsel for the state,' added Nels Gudmundsson, 'has proceeded on the assumption that you will be open, ladies and gentlemen, to an argument based on the hatred of another's race. He has asked you to look closely at the face of the defendant, presuming that because the accused man is a Japanese American you will see an enemy there. After all, it is not so long since our country was at war with the Land of the Rising Sun and its frighteningly well-trained soldiers. You all remember the war films. You all remember the horrors of those years; Mr Hooks is depending on that. He is depending on you to act on feelings best left to a war of ten years ago. He is depending on you to remember this war and to see Kabuo Miyamoto as somehow connected with it. And, ladies and gentlemen,' Nels Gudmundsson whispered, 'let us recall that Kabuo Miyamoto *is* connected with it. He is a respected officer of the United States Army who fought for his country, the United States, in Europe. If you see in his face a lack of emotion, if you see in him a silent pride, it is the pride and hollowness of a soldier who has returned home to this. He has returned to find himself the victim of race hatred – make no mistake about it, this trial is about hatred – in the country he fought to defend.

'Ladies and gentlemen, there are things in this universe that we cannot control, and then there are the things we can. Your task as you discuss this trial is to remember that human beings must act on reason. And so the shape of Kabuo Miyamoto's eyes, the country of his parents' birth – these things must not influence your decision. You must sentence him simply as an American, equal in the eyes of our legal system to every other American. This is what you've been called here to do. This is what you must do.

'I am an old man,' Nels Gudmundsson continued, moving nearer to the jurors and leaning toward them. 'Why do I say this? I say this because as an older man I think about matters in the light of death in a way that you do not. I am like a traveller from Mars who looks down in disbelief at what passes here. And what I see is the same human weakness passed from century to century. What I see is again and again the same sad human weakness. We hate one another; we are the victims of emotions and fears. And there is nothing in human history to suggest we are going to change this. In the face of such a world you have only yourselves to rely on. You have only the decision you must make, each of you, alone. In making your decision, will you stand up against this terrible history and in the face of it be truly human? In God's name, in the name of all that is human, do your duty as jurors. Find Kabuo Miyamoto innocent and let him go home to his family. Return this man to his wife and children. Set him free, as you must.'

In this way the trial of Kabuo Miyamoto ended. The prosecution and the defence had both had their say and their battle was over. The last person to speak was Judge Lew Fielding. His task was to remind the jurors that the charge against the accused man was that of first-degree murder, murder that has been carefully planned and carried out. If they felt that Kabuo Miyamoto had acted in this way, he was guilty. If, however, they had any reasonable doubt about his guilt, they were under an obligation to find him innocent, no matter what other crime they thought he had committed.

The judge paused and let his words sink in. He let his eyes meet and hold the eyes of each juror in turn.

'Ladies and gentlemen,' he said, 'since this is a criminal trial, understand that your decision, whether guilty or not so, must be one on which you all agree. It cannot be based on a majority vote. There is no need for you to hurry or for anyone to feel that they are holding up the rest of us as you discuss your decision. The court thanks you in advance for having served in this trial. The power has gone out and you have passed difficult nights at the Amity Harbor Hotel. It has not been easy for you to concentrate on these proceedings while you are worried about the conditions of your homes, your families and your loved ones. The storm,' said the judge, 'is beyond our control, but the outcome of this trial is not. The outcome of this trial depends on you now. You may leave the courtroom.'

Chapter 23   After the Storm

At three o'clock in the afternoon the jurors in the trial of Kabuo Miyamoto left the courtroom. Two of the reporters leaned their chairs back and sat with their hands behind their heads, relaxing and talking quietly to one another. Abel Martinson allowed Hatsue to speak briefly to the accused man before taking his prisoner out of the court. 'You're going to be free,' she said to Kabuo. 'They'll do the right thing, you'll see.'

'I don't know,' her husband replied. 'But either way, I love you, Hatsue. Tell the kids I love them, too.'

Ishmael Chambers still sat in the courtroom reading over his notes, looking up every now and again to glance at Hatsue Miyamoto. Listening to her speak that morning, he'd been painfully aware of his private knowledge of this woman: he'd understood what each expression suggested, what each pause meant. What he wanted, he realized now, was to drink in the smell of her and to feel her hair in his hands. This desire was all the stronger because he knew it was impossible, like the wish he had to be whole again and to live a different life.

Philip Milholland's notes were in Ishmael's front trouser pocket, and it was just a matter of standing up, crossing over to a court official, and asking to see Judge Fielding. Then bringing the notes out and unfolding them, and watching the look on the official's face, then taking them back from him again and pushing his way into the judge's chambers. Then Lew Fielding looking down through his glasses, pulling the lamp on his desk a little closer, and at last the judge looking up at him as the weight of Philip Milholland's notes began to press against his mind. The ship came through the Shipping Channel at 1.42. Carl Heine's pocket watch stopped at 1.47. It spoke for itself.

He looked at Hatsue again, where she stood in the middle of a small group of Japanese islanders who whispered softly to one another and looked at their watches and waited. He saw her neat clothes, her hair bound tightly to the back of her head, the plain hat held in her hand. The hand itself, loose and graceful, and the way her feet fitted into her shoes, and the straightness of her back

95

and her true way of standing that had been the thing to move him in the beginning, back when he was just a child. And the taste of salt on her lips that time when for a second he had touched them with his own boy's lips, holding on to his glass-bottomed box. And then all the times he had touched her and the smell of all that cedar . . .

He got up to leave, and as he did so the courtroom lights came on. A kind of cheer went up from the court, an embarrassed, careful island cheer; one of the reporters raised his hands into the air, the court official nodded and smiled. The grey colour that had hung over everything was replaced by a light that seemed brilliant by comparison to what had gone before. 'Electricity,' Nels Gudmundsson said to Ishmael. 'Never knew I'd miss it so much.'

'Go home and get some sleep,' answered Ishmael. 'Turn your heater up.'

Nels closed his case, turned it upright, and set it on the table. 'By the way,' he said suddenly, 'did I ever tell you how much I liked your father? Arthur was one admirable man.'

'Yes,' said Ishmael. 'He was.'

Nels pulled at the skin of his throat, then took his document case in his hand. 'Well,' he said, with his good eye on Ishmael, the other wandering crazily. 'Regards to your mother, she's a wonderful woman. Let's pray for the right decision.'

'Yes,' said Ishmael. 'OK.'

On the way out, Ishmael found himself beside Hisao Imada as they both got into their coats. 'Many thanks for giving to us a help,' Hisao greeted him. 'It make our day much better than walking. We have our many thanks to you.'

They went out into the hallway, where Hatsue waited against the wall, her hands deep in her coat pockets. 'Do you need a ride?' asked Ishmael. 'I'm going out your way again. To my mother's house. I can take you.'

'No,' said Hisao. 'Thank you much. We have made for us a ride.'

Ishmael stood there buttoning his coat with the fingers of his one hand. He did up three buttons, starting at the top, and then he slipped his hand into his trouser pocket and let it rest against Philip Milholland's notes.

'My husband's trial is unfair,' said Hatsue. 'You ought to put that in your father's newspaper, Ishmael, right across the front page. You should use his newspaper to tell the truth, you know. Let the whole island see it isn't right. It's just because we're Japanese.'

'It isn't my father's newspaper,' answered Ishmael. 'It's mine, Hatsue. I run it.' He brought his hand out and with some awkwardness slipped another button into place. 'I'll be at my mother's,' he told her. 'If you want to come and speak to me about this there, that's where you can find me.'

Outside he found that the snow had stopped. A hard winter sunlight came through the clouds, and the north wind blew cold and fast. It seemed colder now than it had been that morning. The eye of the storm, he knew, had passed; the worst of it was behind them – his problem was that although the damage caused by the storm could be cleaned up during the coming weeks, the damage of the last twelve years could not be fixed so easily. He could see it all, beginning with the hollow tree and ending on the beach at Tarawa, all that damage and no way of making things better, it seemed.

The truth now lay in Ishmael's own pocket and he did not know what to do with it. He did not know how to conduct himself, and the way he felt about everything was as foreign to him as the sea breaking over the snowy boats and over the Amity Harbor docks. There was no answer in any of it, not in the boats lying on their sides, not in the trees beaten down by the snow. As the jury debated their decision, Ishmael stood outside the court feeling that the cold had made its way to his heart.

Chapter 24   Ishmael's Decision

The power was not yet on along South Beach, and as Ishmael Chambers drove through the snow he glanced into the candlelit windows of the homes he'd known since childhood. Ishmael found his mother at her kitchen table once again, reading by lamp light and drinking tea. As she had the last evening he stayed, she gave him soup to eat, and he told her how the jurors had not reached a decision and how the lights were on once more in town and how the docks had been destroyed by storm winds. His mother was angered by the possibility that the jurors would be driven by hatred of the Japanese, and she hoped that if they were Ishmael would write against it in his newspaper. Ishmael nodded and agreed with her. Then he suggested they spend the night at his apartment with its electric fire and hot water. His mother shook her head and claimed she was content to wait out at South Beach; they could go to Amity Harbor in the morning if they wanted. So Ishmael filled the heater with firewood and hung his coat in the hall. Philip Milholland's notes stayed in his trouser pocket.

At eight o'clock the power came on again. He went through the house turning off lights and turning up the heaters. He made tea and took it into his father's old study, a room with a view of the water in daylight and of his father's much-loved garden. And he sat in silence at his father's desk, in his father's chair, with a single light on.

At nine o'clock his mother kissed his cheek and said she was going to bed. Ishmael returned to his tea in the study, where he looked at his father's books. His father had been, like his mother, a reader. He never hurried. He did not appear to wish something else. There were his evenings reading by the fire or working slowly at the desk he had made for himself. Ishmael remembered his father at work here, his neatly arranged papers spread out before him, a thick dictionary on a stand, and a heavy black typewriter, the desk lamp pulled down low over the keys. Although Arthur had not liked all the islanders he wrote for, at the same time he loved them deeply. Was such a thing even possible? He hoped for the best from his fellow islanders, he claimed, and trusted God to guide their hearts.

Ishmael understood, sitting in his father's place, how he'd arrived at the same view of things. He was, it occurred to him, his father's son.

Ishmael went up the old stairs to the room he'd slept in for so many years and found again the envelope with Kenny Yamashita's return address, the upside-down stamp, her smooth handwriting. There was the letter written on rice paper. With his one hand it would be possible in seconds to turn Hatsue's letter into dust and destroy its message forever. 'I don't love you, Ishmael . . .'

He read the letter a second time, focusing now on its final words: 'I wish you the very best, Ishmael. Your heart is large and you are gentle and kind, and I know you will do great things in this world. But now I must say goodbye to you. I am going to move on with my life as best I can, and I hope that you will, too.'

But the war, his arm, the course of things, it had all made his heart much smaller. He had not moved on at all. He had not done anything great in the world. He had worked automatically for years now, filling the pages of his newspaper with words, burying himself in whatever was safe. So perhaps that was what her eyes meant now on those rare occasions when she looked at him – he'd become so small, not lived up to who he was. He read her letter another time and understood that she had once admired him, there was something in him she was grateful for even if she could not love him. That was a part of himself he'd lost over the years, that was the part that was gone.

He put the letter away in its box and went down the stairs again. His mother, he found, was asleep in her bed; she looked very old in the light from the hallway, a sleeping cap pulled low on her forehead. Looking at her, he felt more deeply how he would miss her when she was gone. It did not matter whether he agreed with her about God. It was only, instead, that she was his mother and she had not given up on loving him.

Beneath the stars, with his overcoat on, he wandered out into the cold. His feet took their own direction through the cedar woods. Here under the trees the snow was fresh and untouched. The branches of the cedars were hung with it and beyond them the sky lay clear and open, the stars frozen points of light. He followed his feet through the woods, to the hollow cedar tree of his youth.

Ishmael sat inside for a brief time with his coat wrapped tightly around him. He listened to the world turned silent by the snow; there was absolutely nothing to hear. The silence of the world blew steadily in his ears while he came to recognize that he did not belong here, he had no place in the tree any longer. Some much younger people should find this tree, hold to it tightly as their deepest secret, as he and Hatsue had. For them it might protect them from what he could not stop himself seeing all too clearly: that the world was silent and cold and empty, and that in this lay its terrible beauty.

He got up and walked and came out of the woods and into the Imadas' fields. The way was clear between the rows of buried strawberries and he followed it with the starlight striking off the snow. And finally he was at the Imadas' door and then in the Imadas' living room, sitting with Hatsue and her mother and father where he had never been before.

Hatsue sat beside him, just beside him, close, wearing a nightdress and her father's old coat, her hair falling like water down her back. And he reached into his pocket and unfolded the notes Philip Milholland had written on 16th September, and Ishmael explained the significance of what the man had written, and why he had come at 10.30 in the night to speak to her after all these years.

Chapter 25   The Real Story

There was no way to call Lew Fielding with the news because the phones were all dead along South Beach. So the four of them, cups of green tea in hand, spoke quietly about the trial of Kabuo Miyamoto, which was for them the only subject possible, as it had been for many days. It was late now, the room very warm, the world outside frozen and bathed in starlight. Fujiko refilled Ishmael's teacup carefully and asked how his mother was. Finally Hatsue's baby began to cry – they could hear him plainly from one of the back rooms – and Fujiko disappeared.

Just after midnight Ishmael said goodbye, shaking hands with Hisao and thanking him for the tea and asking him to thank Fujiko, too. Then he went out. Hatsue followed him out to the door, wearing rubber boots and the old coat of her father's, her hands deep in her pockets now, the fog of her breath hanging in the air around her face. 'Ishmael,' she said, 'I'm grateful.'

'Look,' he replied, 'when you're old and thinking back on things, I hope you'll remember me just a little. I–'

'Yes,' said Hatsue. 'I will.'

She moved closer then, and with her hands still buried deep in her pockets kissed him so softly it was like a whisper against his cheekbone. 'Find someone to marry,' she said to him. 'Have children, Ishmael. Live.'

In the morning his mother woke him at 6.50, saying that the wife of the accused man was here, waiting for him in the kitchen. When he came down Hatsue was at the table drinking coffee, and when he saw her he remembered once again how softly she had kissed him the night before.

'I thought about it all night,' said Hatsue. 'Do you remember when my husband spoke in court? He said that Carl had a lamp up. An oil lamp tied to his mast – that he'd put it there because his lights weren't working.'

Hatsue rubbed her hands together, then separated them again, lightly. 'My idea,' she said to Ishmael, 'is that if that lamp's still up there, right now, wouldn't it mean his batteries really were dead? Supposing you looked up Carl's mast and saw an oil lamp tied up there, just like Kabuo said. Wouldn't that prove something?'

Ishmael sat down on the edge of his father's desk and thought about it. Art Moran's report, the way he recalled it, hadn't said a word about an oil lamp tied high in Carl's mast, but on the other hand Art could have missed it. Such a thing was possible. Anyway, it was worth finding out.

'All right,' said Ishmael. 'Let's go into town. Let's go in and have a look.'

As they drove she was silent for a long time, watching him. She looked at him closely and pulled her hair down over her shoulder. 'You knew about that ship,' she said finally. 'It wasn't something new, was it?'

'A day,' answered Ishmael. 'I had the information for a day. I didn't know what I should do.'

She said nothing in the face of this and he turned towards her silence to see what it might mean. 'I'm sorry,' he said. 'It's inexcusable.'

'I understand it,' answered Hatsue.

At the sheriff's office in Amity Harbor they found Art Moran and explained their idea of what might have happened. At first he was unwilling to accept what they were saying, but after he had read the coastguard notes he agreed to go and look at the boat, although he insisted that Hatsue stayed back at the office – she was too closely involved.

The boats had sat in the waterside storeroom that the sheriff's office had rented since 17th September. Abel opened the sea doors wide and a grey light flooded in. Ishmael looked immediately at the *Susan Marie's* mast. No lamp hung anywhere. Then Abel looked up.

'Hold your light still,' he said. 'Just there.'

Ishmael and Abel directed their lights upward then, so that the two beams shone against the mast now. There were cut pieces of string visible there, loose ends hanging, cut through cleanly on an angle.

'That's where his lamp was hung,' said Ishmael. 'He'd hung a lamp up there, tied it up, because all his lights were dead. That's where Carl hung his lamp.'

'We never took no lamp down,' said Art. 'What are you talking about?'

Abel Martinson climbed up closer and shone his light upward one more time. 'Mr Chambers is right,' he said.

'Listen,' said the sheriff. 'Abel, climb up higher if you can and take a closer look. And don't touch anything.'

'You can see where the string was holding something metal, there's marks of metal here like it could be off the handle of a lamp, maybe. Where the handle rubbed against the string.'

'Anything else?' said the sheriff.

'You can see where the string's been cut,' observed Abel. 'Somebody took a knife to it. And, something else – this stuff on the mast? It looks like it might be blood.'

'From his hand,' said Ishmael. 'He cut his hand. It was in the coroner's report.'

'There's blood on the mast,' said Abel. 'Not much, but I think it's blood.'

'He cut his hand,' repeated Ishmael. 'He cut his hand making room for Kabuo's battery. Then he got his power back up. Then he climbed up there to take his lamp down because he didn't need it any more.'

The deputy slid down and landed hard. 'What's all this about?' he said.

'Something else,' said Ishmael. 'You remember what Horace said? He said Carl had a ball of string in one pocket and an empty knife holder tied to his belt. You remember Horace saying so, Sheriff? How the knife holder was empty?'

'He climbed up to take his lamp down,' said Abel. 'That ship came along and knocked him from the mast. The knife and the lamp went into the water with him. The knife and the lamp were never found, right? And—'

'Quiet a minute, Abel,' said Art Moran. 'I can hardly hear myself think.'

'He hit his head on something,' said Abel. 'The big wave from the ship hit him, the boat rolled over, and then he fell and hit his head on something and slid off, out of the boat.'

Ten minutes later, on the left side of the boat, just below the mast, they found a small break in the wood. Three small hairs were caught in the crack, and Art Moran cut them free with his pocketknife. They looked at the hairs and then they all fell silent.

'We'll take these up to Horace,' decided Art. 'If they end up to be from Carl Heine's head, the judge will have to take things from there.'

At ten o'clock Judge Fielding sat down with Alvin Hooks and Nels Gudmundsson. At 10.45 the jurors were told that they were released from any further duties – the charges against the accused man had been dismissed; new evidence had come to light. The accused man himself was set free immediately and walked out of his cell; standing just outside its door, he kissed his wife for a long time. Ishmael Chambers took a photograph of this; he watched their kiss through his camera. Then he went back to his office, turned up the heat, and loaded paper in his typewriter. And he sat staring at it for some time.

Ishmael Chambers tried to imagine the truth of what had

happened. He shut his eyes and made himself see everything clearly.

The *Susan Marie* had gone dead in the water on the night of 15th September. Carl Heine must have sworn at his misfortune. Then he lit his lamp, slipped a ball of string into his back pocket, and pulled himself up to the top section of the mast. The cotton string he used for net-mending bound the lamp to the mast easily. He hung for a moment and knew that his light was of little use against the fog; nevertheless he set the flame higher before coming down. And he stood listening, perhaps, with the fog closed in around him. It was then that he heard a boat not far off, the sound of a fog-horn blown deliberately. When it was less than one hundred yards away he sounded his air-horn once.

The *Islander* and the *Susan Marie* came together in the fog. Kabuo tied his boat to Carl's. A battery changed hands; it was too large, so a metal holder was beaten back. Carl's hand was cut, there was blood on Kabuo's fishing gaff. An agreement was arrived at. The things that needed to be said were said between them, and Kabuo pushed off into the night.

Maybe it had seemed to Kabuo Miyamoto, alone on the sea so soon afterwards, a fortunate thing to have met Carl Heine in circumstances such as these. Perhaps it had seemed just the start of the luck he'd long thought he needed. His dream, after all, was close to him now, so close that while he fished he must have imagined it: his strawberry land, his children, Hatsue, his happiness. And all the while he was thinking this way, celebrating this sudden good fortune in his life, the noise of the steam whistle from the S.S. *Corona* grew louder and came closer with each moment. And a half-mile to the south and west of the *Islander* Carl Heine stood in his boat and listened uncertainly to the same whistle now coming through the fog. He had made black coffee and held his cup in one hand. His net was out and running true behind as far as he could tell. All of his lights were burning strong now, and the *Susan Marie* ran hard and steady. It was twenty minutes before two o'clock in the morning, enough time left to catch plenty of fish; the coffee would keep him awake long enough to fill up with salmon.

Carl had tried listening into the fog, but the noise of his own engines cut out all other sounds, and he had to shut down the motor. He stood again listening and waiting. At last the steam whistle blew again, closer this time, definitely drawing closer, and he put his coffee cup on to the table. He went outside then and thought about how it would be when the big wave in front of the ship hit his boat, and it seemed to him he was ready to take it, everything was in its place.

Except the lamp tied to the mast. The sudden roll a big ship would cause would break it to pieces, Carl would have seen it that way. And he paid for his desire to avoid waste. With the *Corona* coming down on him in the foggy night, he thought he needed less than thirty seconds to get himself up his mast. Save a lamp that way. What were the risks? Does a man ever believe in his own death or in the possibility of accident?

And so because he was who he was, his mother's son, tidy by nature – he climbed his mast. He climbed it and in doing so opened the cut in his hand he'd got when banging against the battery holder with Kabuo Miyamoto's gaff. Now he hung from the mast, bleeding and listening into the fog, working his knife from its holder. Again there came the noise of the whistle, the low sound of a ship's engines, over to the left. Carl cut through the string he'd tied a few hours earlier, and came away with the lamp held in his fingers.

It must have been that in the fog that night he never saw the wall of water the *Corona* threw at him. The sea rose up from behind the fog and pushed underneath the *Susan Marie* so that the coffee cup on the cabin table fell to the floor, and the movement high up the mast was enough to throw off the man

106

who hung there, not understanding the nature of what was happening, and still he did not see his death coming. His bloody hand lost its hold on the mast, his arms flew out and his fingers opened, letting the lamp and the knife fall into the water, and Carl Heine fell, too, quick and hard against the wooden side of the *Susan Marie*. His head cracked open above the left ear and then he slid heavily beneath the waves, water coming into his watch, stopping it at 1.47. The *Susan Marie* rocked for a full five minutes and, while gradually she settled once again, the body of her captain settled, too, into his salmon net. He hung there in the sea and his boat moved in the water, brightly lit and silent in the fog.

The wall of water moved on. It travelled a half-mile speedily and then gathered beneath the *Islander* so that Kabuo felt it, too. It travelled with nothing more to interrupt it and broke against the shore of Lanheedron Island just before two o'clock in the morning. The whistle of the ship sounded again in the fog. Kabuo Miyamoto, his net in the water, his radio off, the fog as thick as cotton around him, replaced the rope he'd left on Carl's boat with a spare.

And so Kabuo Miyamoto came home to tell his wife how their lives had changed; Philip Milholland finished writing his notes and threw himself into sleep. And later that day Art Moran made his arrest.

Well, thought Ishmael, bending over his typewriter, his fingertips above the keys: Kabuo Miyamoto's heart was unknowable finally. And Hatsue's heart was also unknowable, as was Carl Heine's. The heart of any other, because it had a will, would remain ever mysterious.

Ishmael gave himself to the writing of it, and as he did so he understood this, too: that accident ruled every corner of the universe except the chambers of the human heart.

ACTIVITIES

Chapters 1–3

Before you read

1 Look at the Word List at the back of the book. Find words that are connected with:
   a fishing and the sea
   b plants and the land
   c court trials and the law
2 Read the Introduction to the book and answer these questions.
   a Where does this story take place?
   b Who lives there?
   c What work do these people do?

While you read

3 Write the names of these people.
   a The accused man   ....
   b The dead man   ....
   c The local reporter   ....
   d The accused man's wife   ....
   e The county sheriff   ....
   f The deputy sheriff   ....
   g The defence lawyer   ....

After you read

4 What do you know about:
   a where Carl Heine's body was found?
   b the weather on the night of 15th September?
   c the lights on the *Susan Marie*?
   d the engine of the *Susan Marie*?
   e the batteries on the *Susan Marie*?
   f the batteries on Kabuo Miyamoto's boat, the *Islander*?

Chapters 4–5

Before you read

5 Discuss what you know about Ishmael Chambers.

While you read

6 Are these sentences true (✓) or false (✗)?

    a Ishmael Chambers was injured in the war.   .....

    b After the war, he found it difficult to settle in San Piedro.   .....

    c Ishmael expects the sheriff to lie to him.   .....

    d The sheriff is sure that Carl Heine was murdered.   .....

7 What does Horace Whaley do with these as he examines Carl? Make notes.

    a Carl's clothes

    ....

    b His right leg

    ....

    c His stomach

    ....

    d His head

    ....

    e His skull

    ....

After you read

8 Discuss Whaley's ideas about how Carl Heine might have died.

    a How sure is he?

    b Can he prove them?

    c How persuasive are they to you?

Chapters 6–7

Before you read

9 Discuss how body language and facial expressions differ between people of different nationalities and backgrounds. Give examples from people you know.

While you read

10 Write questions that have the following answers.

    a ....

    Like an enemy soldier.

    b ....

    So that she would not forget she was Japanese.

    c ....

    At a camp where Japanese Americans were held during the war.

    d ....

    How she had kissed Ishmael Chambers.

    e ....

    Eight days later.

    f ....

    That he would love Hatsue for ever.

    g ....

    In the hollow cedar tree.

After you read

11 Discuss these questions.

    a Why did Hatsue and Ishmael keep their friendship secret?

    b What does that tell us about the people who lived on San Piedro?

Chapters 8–9

Before you read

12 People on San Piedro come from families who arrived there from a number of other countries. Discuss these questions.

    a How true is this of the place where you live? Where do recent arrivals come from?

    b What are relations like between new citizens and native residents? If there are problems, what causes them?

While you read

13 What happened first? Number these events in the right order (1–10).

a Kabuo Miyamoto asked Ole Jurgensen to sell him
   the land.   .....
b Ole Jurgensen sold the land to Carl Heine junior.   .....
c The Miyamotos did not make the last two payments.   .....
d Carl Heine senior agreed to sell land to Zenhichi
   Miyamoto, with payments to be made over eight years.   .....
e Carl Heine senior did not intend to take the land back,
   but died.   .....
f Zenhichi Miyamoto offered Carl Heine senior his
   savings.   .....
g Kabuo Miyamoto accused Mrs Etta Heine of stealing
   his land.   .....
h Mrs Etta Heine returned the Miyamotos' money.   .....
i Ole Jurgensen bought the land from Mrs Etta Heine.   .....
j Kabuo Miyamoto said he might talk to Carl Heine
   junior about the land.   .....

After you read

14 Discuss these questions.
    a How would you describe Mrs Heine's character and attitudes?
    b Do you feel sorry for the Miyamotos? Why (not)?

Chapters 10–11

Before you read

15 Past events are very important to the present lives of the people
    of San Piedro. Discuss important events from your own or family
    members' childhood that have affected your life.

While you read

16 Are these sentences true (T) or false (F)?
    a Kabuo fought for the United States.   .....
    b Kabuo and Hatsue fell in love when they were at school.   .....
    c Kabuo's father was a *samurai*.   .....
    d Kabuo became an expert *kendo* fighter.   .....
    e Hatsue's family wanted her to marry a Japanese boy.   .....
    f Hatsue was comfortable with her secret life with Ishmael. .....

After you read

17 Discuss how individuals may be changed by war.

Chapters 12–13

Before you read

18 Find the answers to these questions in the Introduction.
  a Where is Pearl Harbor?
  b When did the Japanese attack it?
  c What happened as a result of the attack?

While you read

19 Complete these sentences.
  After war was declared,
  a the banks refused to ....
  b Art Chambers was criticized for ....
  c Hatsue's father was arrested by ....
  d Hatsue realized that what she felt for Ishmael was ....
  ....
  e The Japanese of San Piedro were sent to Manzanar, to live in
  ....
  f Hatsue's sister shows her mother ....

After you read

20 Discuss these questions.
  a Why were Japanese Americans sent to prison camps? Were there alternative solutions, do you think?
  b Why does Hatsue start a relationship with Kabuo, do you think? Are these good reasons?

Chapter 14

Before you read

21 Use reference books or the Internet to find out where the United States army fought in Asia.

22 Why are these important to Ishmael's story? What happens? Write brief notes.

    a The island of Betio ....

    b Admiral Hill ....

    c Rich Hinkle ....

    d Eric Bledsoe ....

    e Ernest Testaverde ....

    f Ishmael's own experience ....

After you read

23 Explain these statements.

    a Something was dead inside him.

    b He could not write to Hatsue about love.

    c The landing on Betio was a disaster.

    d Ishmael was one of the lucky ones.

Chapters 15–17

Before you read

24 We already know that Kabuo is being tried for murder. Look at the titles of these three chapters. Then discuss these questions.

    a Why is Kabuo a suspect?

    b What might the murder weapon be?

    c What might blood tests prove?

    d How might Susan Marie Heine's evidence help to prove Kabuo's guilt?

While you read

25 What evidence do these people have against Kabuo?

    a Sheriff Art Moran ....

    b Deputy Abel Martinson ....

    c Dr Whitman ....

    d Sergeant Maples ....

    e Susan Marie Heine ....

26 Who is talking? Who are they talking to? What are they talking about?

    a 'A limited search.'

    b 'In a half-hour you might be in Canada.'

    c 'I do it out of habit.'

    d 'Did you hear any part of their conversation?'

Chapters 18–19

Before you read

27 Discuss these questions.

    a How important is the weather to the people of San Piedro? Why? What effects could it have on the trial?

    b How does the weather in your area compare with the weather there?

While you read

28 Write short answers to these questions.

    a What help does Ishmael need to write about the weather in his paper? ....

    b What help is Ishmael given at the gas station? ....

    c Who is Ishmael able to help on the road out of the town? ....

    d How does Evan Powell help Ishmael? ....

    e What helps Ishmael discover the truth about Carl's death? ....

    f How can Ishmael now help Kabuo? ....

    g Why is it difficult for Ishmael's mother to help her son? ....

    h How is Ishmael planning to help Hatsue? ....

After you read

29 Discuss these decisions. Do you agree with them?

    a Hatsue decides she will not write to Ishmael again.

    b Ishmael decides to write the article Hatsue wanted.

    c Ishmael decides to keep the shipping lane records in his pocket.

Chapters 20–22

Before you read

30 The trial is coming to an end. How can Hatsue help her husband and how can Kabuo try to help himself?

While you read

31 What happened first? Put these events in order (1–4).

    a Kabuo stopped his boat to help Carl. .....

    b Kabuo decided to buy a gill-fishing boat. .....

    c Carl and Kabuo made an agreement. .....

    d Kabuo brought home strawberry plants. .....

After you read

32 Discuss what Nels means when he asks the jury to judge Kabuo as an American.

Chapters 23–25

Before you read

33 Discuss whether you think the jurors will find Kabuo innocent or guilty, and why.

While you read

34 What happens at these times?

    a 3 p.m. ....

    b 8 p.m. ....

    c 10.30 p.m. ....

    d midnight ....

    e 6.50 a.m. ....

    f 10 a.m. ....

    g 10.45 ....

After you read

35 How do you think these people feel at the end of the story?

    a Etta Heine

    b Alvin Hooks

    c Nels Gudmundsson

Writing

36 What does this book tell us about the problems of being a non-white American in the 1940s and 1950s? To what extent do you think the situation has changed since then?

37 Explain how and why the families in this story are influenced by their desire to own land.

38 Ishmael believes that 'accident ruled every corner of the universe'. Give three examples of 'accidents' in the story that almost prevent justice being done. Then explain, with reasons related to the story, whether you agree with his statement.

39 Who do you think is the most unpleasant person in this story? Describe that person and give reasons for your choice.

40 Some of the older people in this story were not born in the United States. How do their ideas and opinions differ from their children's?

41 Use examples from the book to show how the landscape, the sea and the weather are important to this story.

42 Imagine that you are Hatsue. Write a letter to one of your sisters the day after the trial. Explain what has happened and how you feel.

43 Write the article that you imagine Ishmael wrote for his newspaper the day after the trial.

44 Both Kabuo and Ishmael were in the United States army during the Second World War. Compare and contrast the ways in which the two men were affected.

45 Name two officials who take part in the trial. Show how they influence the trial itself.

WORD LIST

acre (n) a unit for measuring an area of land, equal to about 4,047 square metres

cabin (n) a small room on a ship in which you live or sleep

cedar (n) a tall tree with leaves, shaped like needles, that do not fall off in winter

chamber (n) a hollow place inside the body of a person or animal

coroner (n) an official who is responsible for discovering the cause of someone's death, especially if the death is unexpected

counsel (n) a lawyer, or a group of lawyers, who speak for someone in a court of law

deceased (n/adj) **the deceased** someone who has died

defendant (n) the person in a court of law who is accused of a crime

deposit (n) a part of the cost of something you are buying that you pay some time before you pay the rest of it

drip (v) to fall in small drops

emerge (v) to appear or come out from somewhere

folder (n) a large, folded piece of card in which you keep loose papers

gaff (n) a large iron hook attached to a pole, used to catch fish

gill-net (v) to catch fish with a flat net, hung vertically in the water, that allows the fish's head to pass through but not to withdraw

lease (n/v) a legal agreement that allows you to use a land or a building, for example, for a period of time in return for rent

lighthouse (n) a tower with a bright light that warns ships of danger

mast (n) a tall pole on which the sails of a ship are hung

pace (v) to walk first in one direction and then in another many times

precise (adj) exact, clear; correct

prosecute (v) to be the lawyer who is trying to prove in a court of law that someone is guilty of a crime

salmon (n) a large ocean fish with silver skin and pink flesh

saw (n) a tool that has a flat blade with a row of sharp points, used for cutting wood

(sea)gull (n) a common grey and white bird that lives near the sea and has a loud cry

sheriff (n) an elected law officer of a county in the United States

skull (n) the bones of a person's or animal's head

specimen (n) a person that you are describing in a particular way

strawberry (n) a sweet red berry that grows on low plants

transaction (n) a business deal or action; buying or selling something, for example

typeface (n) a group of letters or numbers of the same style and size, used in printing

verdict (n) an official decision that is made in a court of law about whether someone is guilty of a crime

A Room with a View
E.M. Forster

Lucy Honeychurch is a young middle-class English girl. Her life is comfortable and she lives in a protected existence. But her experiences on holiday in Italy show her a different side of life. She learns to look more closely at the people around her and discovers the power of her own heart.

Captain Corelli's Mandolin
Louis de Bernières

This is a great love story set in the tragedy of war. It is 1941. The Italian officer, Captain Corelli, falls in love with Pelagia, a young Greek girl. But Pelagia's fiancé is fighting the Italian army …
Captain Corelli's Mandolin is now a film, starring Nicolas Cage.

Anna Karenina
Leo Tolstoy

Anna Karenina, one of world literature's greatest novels, tells the story of a beautiful young woman who is unhappily married to a man much older than herself. When she falls in love with a handsome young soldier, life suddenly seems wonderful. But real happiness is not so easily found …

There are hundreds of Penguin Readers to choose from – world classics, film adaptations, modern-day crime and adventure, short stories, biographies, American classics, non-fiction, plays ...

For a complete list of all Penguin Readers titles, please contact your local Pearson Longman office or visit our website.

Longman Dictionaries

Express yourself with confidence!

*Longman has led the way in ELT dictionaries since 1935.
We constantly talk to students and teachers around the
world to find out what they need from a learner's dictionary.*

Why choose a Longman dictionary?

Easy to understand

Longman invented the Defining Vocabulary – 2000 of the most
common words which are used to write the definitions in our
dictionaries. So Longman definitions are always clear and easy
to understand.

Real, natural English

All Longman dictionaries contain natural examples taken from
real-life that help explain the meaning of a word and show you
how to use it in context.

Avoid common mistakes

Longman dictionaries are written specially for learners, and we
make sure that you get all the help you need to avoid common
mistakes. We analyse typical learners' mistakes and include
notes on how to avoid them.

Innovative CD-ROMs

Longman are leaders in dictionary CD-ROM innovation. Did
you know that a dictionary CD-ROM includes features to help
improve your pronunciation, help you practice for exams and
improve your writing skills?

**For details of all Longman dictionaries, and to choose
the one that's right for you, visit our website:**

www.longman.com/dictionaries